THE CHRISTMAS SPIRIT

/ / / /

H.P MALLORY
&
J.R. RAIN

THE HAVEN HOLLOW SERIES

Remarkable Remedies

Published by
Rain Press

Printed in the United States of America.

ISBN- 9798370425622

Chapter One
Narrated by Poppy
Christmas Eve

The ring on my finger stared back at me like an accusation.

I turned it around, and around again until it wore a red mark on my skin.

It really was pretty, with a white gold band that looked nice against my pale skin. Yellow gold always looked a bit funny on me, just too much contrast, and not in a good way. But this ring... well, it was lovely, really. The diamond was done in a princess cut that sparkled with rainbows in the smallest amount of light. And the little

1

flecks of sapphire that surrounded the center stone were the exact same shade as my eyes.

The ring was elegant, tasteful, and more importantly, obviously picked out with a lot of care for the person who would be wearing it.

Looking at it made me want to cry. And I couldn't quite put my finger on the reason why.

Eager for a distraction, I came around the counter of my store to straighten the shelves for the twentieth time that afternoon. The earlier crowds had decimated my stock, and on any other day, I would have been thrilled with the success. It seemed like potions were the hot ticket Christmas present or stocking stuffer this year which was... well, it was great. And, yet, I didn't feel great. Staring at the cheerfully decorated and nearly barren shelves, I found myself hoping that a mess would appear for me to fix.

Because then at least I could fix something.

It was Christmas Eve, and my shop, 'Poppy's Potions', was set to close early. I wanted a little extra time to get home to my son so we could get in some last-minute holiday festivities before the big day tomorrow.

Finn was growing up so fast, already in his last year of middle school, and I wanted to squeeze in as much time as I could before he got too old to want to hang out with his mom. He was already less excited about the holidays than he used to be (ever since learning Santa wasn't real).

I couldn't help but remember when he was younger how we'd have long debates over what kind of cookies to leave out for Santa, and the plate would end up piled high with chocolate chip, peanut butter, and sugar cookies. Then, in the middle of the night, I'd have to chew on a raw carrot to convince Finn that the reindeer had liked the snack he'd left out for them. One year I'd even gone so far as to leave boot tracks in flour leading from the fireplace to the Christmas tree, in the hopes Finn would believe Santa had tracked in snow (never mind the fact that it didn't snow in Los Angeles).

Lately, he was still excited about the holidays but not like he had been when he was a little boy. Thinking on it now made me nostalgic about his younger years. There was nothing quite like seeing your kid's face light up with the magic of the season.

I shook off the mood. Where Finn was concerned, I had a few more years of holiday movie marathons ahead of us still. No need to worry about things that hadn't even happened yet.

I had plenty of *other* things to worry about.

At least sales had been way better than I'd thought they would be. Looking around at the almost empty shelves was pretty satisfying, even if it meant I was going to have a lot of work ahead of me to restock after the New Year, if not before. I'd even started to brew some of the more popular potions in the shop. I usually worked on them at home, but at least this way, when I had a lull, I could whip up a few things in the interim.

Soon enough, daylight started to fade, the shadows stretching longer, and it was almost time to lock the doors and head home for the evening. I didn't think there would be many more last-minute customers so close to closing time, especially on Christmas Eve, but I'd give it a few more minutes, just in case.

Some of the fake snow I'd laid on the antique wooden shelves had fallen off and was now dusting the floor, so I carefully swept it up and dumped it back onto the shelves. Not only was the snow festive, but it, and the twinkling little fairy lights I'd strung up, had made the rainbow glass of my various potion bottles sparkle like something truly magical.

As I deposited the fake snow back on the shelf, the fairy lights glinted off the engagement ring on my left hand, and my stomach clenched tight again. So much for the distraction.

I cradled my hand to my chest, looking down at the ring as I breathed out a long and dramatic sigh. The guilt was almost suffocating. Why wasn't I happy? Most women would have been ecstatic that their wonderful, caring, handsome boyfriend had proposed. So why was I filled with so much anxiety and this feeling of... being unsettled?

It was true that I hadn't had the best luck with relationships in the past, but I didn't think that was what was causing my disquiet. Because even though all my other relationships had been disasters, Marty was different. There was nothing about him that in any way mirrored the jerkoffs I'd dated in the past. He was sweet, and caring, and a little goofy, true, but an overall good guy. No, he was a *great* guy.

And yet… why did I feel like there was an anvil in my stomach when I thought about marrying him? Was this just fear speaking? Nerves?

It was the exact same feeling I'd had when he'd proposed the night of Thanksgiving dinner when we'd been surrounded by friends and family. He'd asked, and I'd blurted 'yes' without much more thought. Well, those thoughts were making themselves known with a vengeance now, and they had my stomach turning into knots like I'd had too much caffeine.

I just kept picturing the look on Andre's face… Andre, the man who had stormed into my life and turned it upside down before storming back out again. Except, he'd returned most recently, and his return had plopped my life right back into 'topsy-turvy' territory again. But the expression on Andre's face that night, the moment Marty had popped the question—it had been… blank. Shocked, yes, but something more still, yet I couldn't put my finger on what that something more had been.

Not that it really mattered because Andre and I were nothing to each other—really little more than acquaintances. He'd been throwing around the idea of training Finn in Magician magic but that idea had crumbled the moment Andre had to return to Portland. And ever since Thanksgiving dinner, when I'd agreed to become Marty's wife, I hadn't seen nor heard from Andre. I wasn't even sure if he was still in Haven Hollow or if he'd already returned to Portland. Furthermore, I doubted I'd ever see him again—he appeared to be the quintessential bachelor—a man who'd never been married and didn't settle down in any one spot for more than a blink. Yes, there had been something electric between us, but whatever that thing was, it didn't matter now.

Okay, enough about Andre.

I took a deep breath, and tried to stop my stomach from jittering as I focused on the main issue littering my tormented thoughts at the moment—why was I feeling so unsettled about this engagement? When I was working up a new potion recipe, it really helped me to take notes, to list everything out inside my head—things like what I wanted the potion to do, what ingredients I'd need, what I intended to focus on in order to imbue it with Gypsy magic. Things like that.

So, being the methodical person I was, I thought I should make a list in this case, as well. At least a list in my head. Maybe that would help me sort out these troubling feelings so I could get to the root of what was bothering me.

Here went nothing…

Pro: Marty was kind and thoughtful.

Con: he could be a little scatterbrained.

Pro: he got along great with Finn and the two really cared about each other.

Con: he could be a little childish at times. In fact, sometimes it felt like I had two kids, not one.

Pro: we got along great, and I couldn't remember a time we'd actually argued, anything more than a minor tiff or disagreement, anyway. We were best friends.

Con: he *felt* like my best friend, and our relationship didn't really feel… romantic or sensual. And the sex? Hmm, I didn't really want to think about the sex.

Con: sometimes he did things without thinking.

Con...

I just wasn't in love with him.

The last one stood out in my mind like someone had written it across my thoughts in glowing neon ink. I buried my head in my hands with a groan.

I did love Marty; I did. He was my best friend, next to Wanda. But love him romantically, passionately, intensely with the sort of sexual desire that was supposed to exist in a romantic relationship? That was a different thing entirely.

But physical passion fades, I reminded myself. *And when it does, wouldn't you rather be left with a great friend? Someone you could build a life with? Someone who has similar goals?*

Yes, yes, and yes.

Not to mention the fact that when it came to relationships and love, I didn't exactly have a good track record. In fact, with the exception of Marty and Roy, I'd dated a string of losers. Cheaters, liars, users.

And Marty wasn't any of those things. He was sincere and kind and funny.

Then stop worrying about it, I told myself resolutely. *Break your track record and let yourself be happy for once. You know you can be happy with Marty…*

An image of Andre sitting at my dinner table that night dropped into my head like a bomb and I had to chase the memory away. Angrily.

Will you stop thinking about him! I yelled at myself at the exact moment the bell over the door rang softly, and I jerked my head up. Plastering my most welcoming customer service smile on, I pushed my turbulent thoughts to the back of my head and focused on my customer.

The woman wasn't anyone I'd seen before. Haven Hollow certainly wasn't a large town, but it was big enough that I didn't know everyone, not to mention the fact that it was also a pretty big tourist destination. Especially this time of year.

"Hello and welcome to Poppy's Potions!" I called out and offered my visitor a friendly wave. "I'm Poppy, so just let me know if you need help with anything."

She smiled, and I was struck by how pretty she was. Loose curls hung over the shoulders of her scarlet coat, so pale a blond that they were actually platinum. Her eyes were a bright, lively green that you didn't usually see without the help of colored contact lenses. Above those round and big eyes were narrowly defined eyebrows with a perfect arch. Her face was heart-shaped and with her alabaster skin, button nose, and pink lips, she looked like one of those expensive, porcelain dolls. Snow from outside dusted her coat and hair, glittering in the overhead lights of the shop.

She looked at me and her smile broadened, making her look like a little girl, almost. If I'd had to guess her age, I would have put her in her early twenties. "Merry Christmas Eve."

"Merry Christmas Eve to you too!"

The woman turned then, almost spinning as she took in the entire store, the skirt of her long coat flaring out around her green dress and matching green tights that ended in high black, leather boots with a clunky heel.

"What a sweet shop!" She hurried over to the nearest shelf, examining the colored fairy lights and fake snow, tilting her head to see the way the potion bottles reflected the light. She seemed to delight in the display and turned to smile at me, her grin complete with dimples. "It's like one of those old-fashioned stores you see in the movies."

"Thanks." I couldn't help but smile in response, the tight knot of distress that was wedged up behind my ribs easing a little bit in the face of her honest excitement. "I'm so glad you like it."

"I just love this time of year," the young woman almost sang as she turned to face me then and walked right up to the counter, glancing at all the baskets of odds and ends as she shuffled through them, seemingly more delighted with each new bobble. "I'm Noelle, by the way."

"It's nice to meet you, Noelle. I'm Poppy… like I said."

Noelle laughed, and the sound chimed like little silver bells. "Wonderful!" Then she put the miniature snow globe she'd been holding back on the counter and turned to face me with those bright green, curious eyes. "I was hoping you might be able to help me with something, Poppy."

"Of course." I smoothed the front of my

festive llama Christmas sweater down and headed towards the counter. "Were you looking for something specific?"

Noelle skipped forward, the movement looking almost like a dance as she put her gloved hands on the counter, looking eager. "I am…" Then she breathed in deeply and frowned which seemed to be an odd expression on her. "It's a bit of a long shot, but you wouldn't happen to have any *Holiday Cheer* potions in stock, would you?"

My heart sank a little. I hated to disappoint a customer, especially on Christmas Eve. "I don't say this often," I started, a little perplexed, "But I've actually never heard of that potion before."

I had to admit, I was a little curious. I had a pretty extensive knowledge of potions, having been trained in the art of brewing potions from the time I was a little girl. Not to mention the huge amount of recipes I'd inherited from my family. It wasn't often I came across one I'd never even heard of but whenever I did, I was eager to find out whatever I could about it.

"Ah, I was afraid of that." Noelle's shoulders sagged a little, disappointment tugging the corners of her mouth down even further.

"Can you tell me about it?"

She nodded. "It was something my grandmother used to make, and ever since she moved on to the great beyond," she paused and looked upward, winking at my ceiling as if her grandmother were hovering there (and who knew? Maybe she was), "I've been trying to find someone who knows the recipe."

"What's *Holiday Cheer* potion meant to do?" I started, with a little laugh. "I mean, beyond the obvious."

Noelle laughed that bell-like sound again. "Well, it's meant to help make holiday wishes come true."

I hated to disappoint her, and not just because I was losing out on a sale. Memories were important, especially when they were all we had left of a loved one. I would've delighted in being able to give Noelle that little bit of nostalgia for her grandmother.

"I'm sorry," I said, and meant it. "I wouldn't even know what to put in it."

Noelle tapped one holly red nail against her lips, thinking hard enough for a little wrinkle to form between her eyebrows. "You know," she started slowly. "I have my grandmother's recipe."

"Oh," I started as she nodded and the frown dropped right off her face, to be replaced with another hopeful and happy smile. This Noelle had to be the cheeriest person I'd ever met.

"The problem is—I just don't have any talent for brewing potions." Then her smile broadened as she did another tinkling laugh. "Maybe we can make a deal."

"A deal?"

She nodded and her curls bounced with her renewed enthusiasm. "How about I give you the recipe, and in exchange, you make a bottle for me?" She glanced around the store again. "And I don't mind at all if you decide to bottle it up and sell it. Everyone can do with some holiday cheer!"

"Truer words have never been spoken," I answered on a laugh, thinking I should be first in line with the crappy attitude I'd been hosting lately.

But at the thought of a new potion recipe, excitement fizzled through me like champagne bubbles. Potion makers tended to horde our recipes. They were passed down through the generations like family heirlooms, so the chance of learning a new one was something I couldn't pass up, not to mention I was beyond happy to be able to help Noelle.

"Then you'll help me?" Noelle asked.

"Sure, I'd love to."

Noelle clapped her hands in excitement. "Wonderful!" Then she tugged a notebook and a pen decorated to look like a snowman out of her purse, and started scribbling what I imagined was the recipe which surprised me because I figured she'd have to leave and come back with it, but apparently not so.

I stepped closer to the counter as I listened to her name off the ingredients as she wrote them down.

"One half part Bayberry, one eighth part Clove, one eighth part Cinnamon," she sang out. "One eighth part Pine and one eighth part Peppermint."

"As far as the potion making goes, does *Holiday Cheer* require a certain moon phase or a specific day of the week on which to brew it?" I asked.

She looked up from her notebook at me.

"Nope!"

As I came closer, a sweet scent reached my nose. I wasn't sure what perfume Noelle was wearing, but it reminded me of the scent of baking shortbread or maybe sugar cookies.

"The only thing it requires is that it be decanted in the days leading up to Christmas," Noelle continued and as she smiled at me, I was struck by how easy the recipe was —and all the ingredients I actually had on hand—in the store! "And what better day to brew it than Christmas Eve, when the magic of Christmas is at its peak!" she finished.

I nodded, because I could feel the holiday magic all around us.

Noelle finished writing, then tore the paper from her notebook and handed it to me with a flourish and a huge grin as I glanced over the steps and the ingredients once more, just to make sure it was as simple as it appeared to be.

"Great!" I said as I glanced up at her again. "It should only take about twenty minutes or so."

"Perfect."

"Do you want to poke into some of the

other stores on Main Street while I work on it?" Then I cocked my head to the side as I thought better of the suggestion. "I'm not sure they'll all still be open…"

Noelle loosened her green scarf a little. "Is it alright if I wait here?"

"Of course."

"I'll have fun looking through all your shelves."

I laughed. "Unfortunately, they're mostly bare at the moment but the potion won't take long." As to the potion itself, I was excited about it. Something to help holiday wishes come true? Yes, please. If it worked, I'd have to think about stocking it for next year.

It only took me a few seconds to collect and arrange all the ingredients from the storage room in the back. After I placed them into a small basket and carried them to the front counter, I couldn't help my smile as Noelle hummed 'It's beginning to look a lot like Christmas' and I hummed along with her.

My fingers glanced over the bottles of my carrier oils, and I decided on almond, figuring the sweet scent would complement the warm notes of the cinnamon and clove.

And then I started.

I lost myself in the brewing, my hands moving almost on instinct as I checked the directions and rechecked the measurements, being careful with each ingredient to make sure I got the ratios perfect, all the while keeping in mind the feeling and the magic of the holiday season. When creating potions, *intention* was the foremost ingredient. It was the thought that empowered the magic.

Once everything was combined, I grabbed a couple of pretty green bottles and funneled the potion inside them. Why was I making two? I figured I'd give the recipe a try as well, just in case I wanted to start offering *Holiday Cheer* as part of my Christmas line next year. And if I got bitten by the holiday bug? All the better—if anyone could have used a little de-Grinching—it was me.

It actually took less time to brew the potion than I thought it would, and when I glanced up to let Noelle know as much, I felt my smile falter because she was gone. I blinked in confusion, the potion bottles still in my hands as I wondered where in the world she could have disappeared to. I'd never heard the bell over the door chime so it wasn't as though she'd walked out of the store and yet… the store was empty, save myself. There wasn't a single shred of red wool or a silver curl to be seen or a lilting, little laugh to be heard.

Maybe she'd gotten a phone call and had to leave and I was just so deep into my potion making, that I hadn't heard the bell over the door as she walked out? That had to be the case because it was the only thing that made any sense. Of course, when it came to Haven Hollow and incidences of the weird, things that didn't make sense seemed to be a regular occurrence. For all I knew, I might have just been visited by a ghost.

But she hadn't looked like a ghost and I would know—I'd seen and dealt with plenty of them.

Disappointed, I moved over to the counter to set the bottles down, when something caught my eye. There was a candy cane lying on the dark wood of the counter. Still wrapped in cellophane, with the paper tag from Sweeter Haunts, the Halloween themed candy store just up the street. The candy cane was pretty, with perfect red and white stripes, and a delicate ribbon of green swirling through it. I could practically taste that fresh burst of peppermint just looking at it.

Noelle must have left it before she'd walked out. Hmm…

I shrugged, feeling a little sad that I hadn't been able to give her the potion she'd come for, but I figured she'd return just as soon as her phone call, or whatever had called her away, ended. I slipped one of the bottles beneath the counter with the candy cane, hoping she'd be back soon because I was closing up in another twenty minutes or so.

Putting my own bottle of *Holiday Cheer* into my coat pocket, I walked to the front of the store, flipped the sign on the door to 'closed', before glancing up and down the street to see if there was any sign of her. But nope, nothing but an empty and snowy street greeted me. As I watched, the lamps along Main Street lit up, making the snow reflect the light like millions of prisms.

After waiting another twenty minutes, there was still no sign of Noelle so I breathed out a sigh, locked the front door, and then turned off all the lights in the shop as I headed to the back parking lot and my Jeep.

I was excited to get home to Finn and the full night of baking and holiday movies ahead of us.

Chapter Two

The pie came out of the oven with a wash of apple and cinnamon scented air, and I couldn't keep the smile off my face.

Maybe the lattice crust on top was a little darker than I would have liked, but it was still a beautiful pie made with Granny Smith apples from my own backyard. And who didn't like homemade apple pie? In short: no one.

I carried it over to the cooling rack with careful hands and slid it next to the pecan pie that was already sitting there. When I was sure the apple pie was steady, and not about to slip off the kitchen counter, I stripped off my oven mitts and turned to check on Finn.

"How's it going over there?"

"Um." Finn frowned, trying to peel a strip of tape off his fingers without balling it up. The wrapping paper was pinned under his elbow—clearly, he was trying to keep it from rolling back up as he got himself sorted. "I mean, nothing's on fire, so I guess: pretty good."

I laughed and moved to hold the paper in place until Finn was ready to fold the edges up around the box he was wrapping.

He flashed me a smile. "Thanks, Mom."

The big day was tomorrow, and we still had plenty to do.

"Okay," I said when Finn had the paper successfully sealed and the ribbon tied off. "What's next?"

Finn thought about it for a second, glancing through the bags on the chair next to him. "I still need to wrap Astrid's present."

"Okay." I nodded, pretending I didn't notice the way Finn's cars flushed at the mention of Wanda's very pretty red-haired cousin. "Do you think you can handle wrapping her present? I'm going to put the sweet potato casserole together, so I don't have to do it tomorrow."

Finn seemed relieved that I hadn't said anything about his obvious crush on Astrid and nodded. Then he tried to tug something out of the bag next to him, angling his body so I couldn't see what it was.

I left him to it, turning back to the fridge so he couldn't see me smile. Astrid had been helping Finn out with his magic studies, even though she was a witch and he was a Magician, and their powers weren't really that similar. Still, she was giving him a crash course in supernatural history and theory, trying to get as much information into Finn as she could before she went away to university at Blood Rose Academy. I was grateful for her help, because my magic had to do with brewing potions, and as a human with some magical talent, I just didn't have the knowledge that Astrid had been steeped in her entire life.

With any luck, some time in the new year, we could find Finn a mentor who could help him come to terms with what it was to be a Magician. Someone with years of experience and someone who was decidedly *not* Andre, the only actual Magician either of us knew. *But if there was one Magician, there had to be others*, or so I'd firmly told myself. Repeatedly.

I was just searching for a potato peeler in the jumble of stuff that had taken over the utensil drawer when my phone chimed with an incoming text. I fished it out of my pocket, and my heart sank a little when I saw it was from Marty.

Merry Christmas Eve, the text read, followed by a half a dozen exclamation points and a series of holiday emoji faces.

Merry Christmas Eve, I typed back. Then there was the sign of three asterisks as Marty typed his response.

I'll be by first thing in the morning, since I think Santa might be leaving a few things here for you and Finn. I'll be headed to Taliyah's place in the afternoon to celebrate with the boys and Aunt Joan and Uncle James. Do you want to come along?

Are we invited? I texted back.

Of course! Wherever I'm invited, you guys are invited.

I smiled as I read the message. I could practically hear Marty's voice in my head.

Okay, let me check with Finn? But don't forget Christmas dinner with my crazy uncles at 6.

How could I forget? I love those guys! Can't wait to see you! Love you!

I couldn't bring myself to actually write the words so I responded with three hearts and a smiley face.

Don't get me wrong, I was really looking forward to Christmas morning with Marty and Finn, my two favorite men in the whole world. But part of me was a little worried about seeing Marty again. We hadn't really gotten to spend a lot of time together since he'd proposed, between my recovery from fighting off a bunch of winter faeries that had attacked the town, and then all the holiday excitement. Not to mention Marty's side business as a ghost buster. I wasn't sure why, but his business got really busy around this time of year. Halloween made sense, but Christmas? I guessed it was kind of a traditional ghost time of year.

And, of course, that thought led to thoughts about Noelle and how she'd just disappeared from the store earlier. I couldn't help but wonder if she'd returned to find the place all locked up. Oh, well, hopefully she'd come back on the twenty-sixth and I could give her the *Holiday Cheer* potion then.

But back to Marty and seeing him in the morning, I just wasn't sure what to expect, or how to act. I didn't want to make him feel bad, but I was still wrestling with this never-ending doubt that had been eating me alive ever since he'd put that ring on my finger. Glancing down at it now, the ring felt very heavy on my hand. I couldn't seem to stop twisting it around and forced myself to stop, before I wore a permanent groove into my finger.

"Okay, done," Finn said, setting aside a small box that was wrapped in deep purple paper, with a silver ribbon tied into a very careful bow. It was clear just how much effort he'd put into wrapping Astrid's gift, since his usual wrapping job looked more like the tape and paper had just survived a war.

I stuffed my phone back into my pocket. "Wow, that's really pretty. I bet Astrid will love it."

Finn's ears flushed dark red again, and

he gave a painfully neutral shrug as he struggled to play it cool. "Yeah."

I had to bite my lip to keep from smiling.

"How about you help me with this casserole before you head to bed?"

"Sure." Finn sprung up from his chair and walked to the cupboard to grab the dish I'd need. "How long is it going to take?" he asked with a frown as he glanced at the clock over the breakfast table. "It's not even nine, Mom."

I grabbed the peeler and the first sweet potato. "The earlier you go to bed, the earlier Santa will come."

Finn rolled his eyes. "Come on, Mom. I'm too old for that stuff."

My heart gave a little twinge, but I made sure to keep a smile on my face. "Hey, you never know. Why can't Santa be real? Everything else in this town is."

Finn thought about that for a minute, cocking his head to one side, before eventually shaking it. "Nah."

I shrugged. "Maybe he's supernatural. We have a Sasquatch, why not Father Christmas?"

Finn shook his head again, but didn't

push the issue. "We should watch a movie when your casserole is done."

My smile pulled a little wider. "Okay. How about we finish up here, and you pick out a Christmas movie? And Die Hard is *not* a Christmas movie," I added hastily.

"Debatable," Finn hummed. "But fine." Then he smiled a huge grin. "How about Clark Griswold?"

"Music to my ears," I answered.

"*'And why is the carpet all wet, Todd!'*" Finn quoted with a laugh.

***

Once Christmas Vacation was over, and Finn had headed off to bed, I stayed up for a bit to clean up the last of the cookie crumbs and wrapping paper scraps. I still needed to put the presents from Santa out underneath the tree and fill Finn and Marty's stockings which were hanging above the fireplace.

Normally, I loved the holidays. All the pretty colors and lights, all the food, and seeing people's faces when they unwrapped a carefully selected present. Not to mention the Christmas carols, and the joy that just kind of drifted through the air. It brought me so much joy to see family and loved ones, all in one place. But this year… well, something just felt off.

And guilt was sitting in my stomach like a lead weight. I just couldn't seem to push all these troubled thoughts to the side. No matter how many times I told myself this was the right decision—that *Marty* was the right decision, the weight in the pit of my stomach remained.

All I wanted was a nice Christmas. To be able to feel that joy, like I normally would any other year. I definitely didn't want my sour mood to drag anyone else down, or worse, make Marty take notice. I didn't want him to worry about me having doubts about marrying him, and certainly not before I had a chance to sort all my thoughts out on my own and yet I wondered how I could act normal when everything inside me felt anything but.

With a sigh, I walked to the coat rack in the hall. With my uncles coming, I figured I'd better put some things away, so everyone would actually have a spot to hang their things up. As I moved my coat to the closet, something in the pocket tinkled, and I remembered the potion I'd stuffed in there earlier. I hung up my coat and fished the little green bottle out.

The bottle of *Holiday Cheer* seemed to smile and wink up at me as I realized I was in definite need of some. No time like the present to test the potion out and see if it was something I wanted to carry at the store.

I took the bottle back to the kitchen and sank down into a chair. The stopper came out of the narrow neck with a little bit of a wiggle, and the warm scent of cinnamon and spice trickled out, laced with the freshness of peppermint and pine. I took a deep breath, letting it fill my lungs and clear my head. The smell alone was almost enough to put me into a festive mood.

Almost.

I used the stopper to dab the oil onto my wrists and throat, right over my pulse points, and then inhaled deeply. The scent really was festive. Closing my eyes, I imagined the potion spreading the holiday feeling all throughout. But then my worries moved in like a proverbial storm cloud.

"I just wish I knew what to do about this

marriage," I sighed as I opened my eyes and slid the stopper back into the bottle.

The lingering aroma of baking and holiday treats followed me up the stairs to my bedroom, and, later, into my dreams.

***

By the time my head hit the pillow, I worried I'd just toss and turn all night.

That without the distractions of all the holiday preparations, it would just be me and my thoughts, going back and forth like they had been for the last month, until the wee hours of the morning.

But whether I'd worried myself out, or it was just owing to all the running around, cleaning, baking, and long work hours, I was asleep in minutes.

Unfortunately, my sleep wasn't very restful.

"I think… you don't love me," Marty accused, from where he was sitting on my couch in front of the Christmas tree. I watched in agony as his face crumpled and my heart slammed against the inside of my ribs like it was trying to break free and es-

cape.

I tried to reach for him, to hold him, to do anything, but the ring on my finger felt like it weighed more than a boulder, pinning me in place. It was so heavy, I found I couldn't move at all.

"Marty," I whispered, tears hot enough to scald a path down my cheek. "Marty, I–"

He shook his head and stood, staring down at me with a heart-breaking look on his face. "It's not fair to marry me if you're not in love with me, Poppy."

I managed to jerk awake, my heart pounding through my chest, and then I just lay there for a long moment, tears sliding down my temples to soak into my pillow. There was a lump in my throat that I could barely breathe around, a burning, choking weight.

The comforting smell of cinnamon managed to lull me back to sleep after a while, but my dreams were full of more of the same. Every time I closed my eyes, all I could see was Marty's devastated face as the truth hit him with full force—I wasn't *in* love with him.

Three more times the nightmares woke

me, before I fell into a kind of exhausted half-doze where I dreamed of fraying red ribbons, and a smooth, British accented voice calling my name.

I blinked myself awake and found I was sitting at my own kitchen table.

The change in scenery startled me so badly, I almost fell off my chair. I looked around myself wildly as I took in the darkness of the night outside and the fact that everything was as I'd left it. Had I been sleepwalking? Had I passed out at the table and just never actually made it to bed in the first place?

But as I glanced around the kitchen, I realized everything *wasn't* exactly as I'd left it. For one, the lights were dim, and there was a mug of hot chocolate sitting in front of me, still steaming gently. At the sound of music, I turned to face a radio I'd never seen before that was sitting on the counter and playing Christmas carols.

What in the world?

I stood up and walked over to the window which immediately frosted as soon as the heat of my breath made contact with the coldness of the pane. In the reflection of the porch light, I could see a gentle snow fall-ing, sparkling under the moonlight. And that was odd because the porch light had burned out and needed to be changed. It was one of the things on my list to address and yet, here it was, burning happily.

"What is going on," I said to myself as I glanced down and found I was dressed in my favorite flannel pajamas, the ones with all the kittens in Santa hats. Everything around me felt cozy, warm and safe and yet, on the inside, I felt anything but.

I ran my hands over the fabric that was covering my thighs. It felt real enough, but these pajamas had been brand new—I'd only purchased them last week—and yet now, as I looked at them, I noticed the fabric was faded and in some areas, the seams were worn.

And that made zero sense.

It's a dream, I realized.

It had to be. But everything was so vivid and clear—so real, like I'd used *Dreamtime Oil* to fall asleep. And yet, I hadn't.

I turned around and walked back to the table, reaching out for the mug of steaming chocolate. I could feel the heat of it on my fingers and when I brought it to my lips, I noticed that even the hot chocolate tasted real and delicious; not too hot, not too sweet, perfectly creamy on my tongue.

When I set the mug back down on the table, I realized I wasn't alone.

In exactly the same way as she'd disappeared in my store, she'd suddenly reappeared in my kitchen. In exactly the span of a blink.

Noelle.

She was sitting across from me. But the boots and coat she'd worn in the shop were gone. Now she was wearing a long, green velvet gown that pooled around her on the kitchen floor. Half of her curls were drawn up artfully, while the rest spilled down over her shoulders, as pale as the snow outside. There were leaves in her hair, a crown made of holly, their bright red berries gleaming in the soft light, looking like little jewels.

She smiled at me like an old friend. "Hello again, Poppy."

"Hello." I glanced around again, noting the small changes in my kitchen—things in places I hadn't left them, other things that I didn't recognize at all. And that foreign radio now belting out *Silent Night*. I glanced out the window to the snowy scene outside before returning my attention to Noelle.

"This is a dream, isn't it? It's not real."

"Well, you're half right." Noelle folded her hands on the table. Each of her nails was polished a deep red with a sheen of silvery glitter on top, her thumbs decorated with little painted holly clusters. "This is a dream. But that doesn't mean it isn't real."

I frowned. "Lucid dreaming—right," I started with a quick nod. I'd had lucid dreams in the past, but usually that was because I *wanted* to have them—I'd prepared to have them. This time, they'd been sprung on me. "Okay. Can I ask why you're in my dream?"

I mean, the Marty ones made a lot of sense. I was more than sure my subconscious was picking up on my stress over this whole engagement. But my dreams after that? Yeah, those had gotten a little abstract, with red ribbons, and a man's voice that I'm pretty sure had been Andre's. I mean, I didn't really know anyone else with a British accent...

Noelle smiled, and in the way of dreams,

it started to snow gently, right there inside my kitchen.

"I think it might be time for a proper introduction," she said.

"A proper introduction?" I shook my head.

She nodded. "Poppy, I'm Noelle, the spirit of Christmas."

I blinked, not sure how to respond to that. "Oh. Well, it's nice to meet you... again."

She huffed her silver bell laugh. "Likewise."

"Um, is there a reason why you're in my kitchen?"

The smile faded from her face, and she reached out slowly to take my hands. Hers were warm. "I'm here to offer you a gift."

"A gift?"

She nodded. "Yes, I heard your Christmas wish, and I came to help."

"My Christmas wish?"

And then I remembered—I remembered how I'd anointed myself with the *Holiday Cheer* potion and then I'd wished I knew what to do about Marty.

I gave Noelle a little, shy smile as I

thought to myself how embarrassing it was that she'd somehow overheard my internal debate over whether or not I should marry Marty. But then I had to catch myself because this was a dream, after all, so I was basically getting embarrassed by my own subconscious which was kind of silly.

"There's a lot of magic in the air at this time of year," Noelle continued as she stood up and turned around to face me in a big sashay of her beautiful gown. "You should consider yourself lucky that I heard your plea, Poppy."

I didn't exactly feel very lucky though. "Is that why you wanted me to make the Holiday Cheer potion—so I'd anoint myself with it?"

She nodded and her curls bobbed up and down with her obvious excitement. "It was the only way to prepare you for your journey."

"My journey?"

Then she held out a hand to me. "Are you ready?"

"For what?"

She laughed. "We are going to take a little trip."

My breath caught in my throat, and I was pretty sure if it wasn't a dream, my heart would have been pounding a mile a minute. "A trip where?"

She nodded and seemed excited about the prospect. "Into your life."

Wait. "I'm not about to get Ebenezer Scrooge'd, am I?" I squinted, suspicious. The last thing I wanted to do was take a spooky trip through my life with a scary ghost. Not that Noelle was scary, but I was worried about the Ghost of Christmas Future, or was it the Ghost of Christmas Past? And I also wasn't exactly thrilled about Marley and his chains. In general, I didn't do well with jump scares.

Noelle burst out laughing as she wiped her eyes, grinning at me. "No. Nothing so sinister. I meant it when I said it was supposed to be a gift."

"Thank you," I breathed. "But, why are you giving this gift to me?"

Even though this was all just the work of my subconscious mind, I decided to go with it. At the very least, maybe it would shed some light on the troubled state of my thoughts lately.

Noelle smiled and patted my hand. "You're a good person, Poppy. And on this most magical of nights, I have the power to help you work your way through the doubt that's been plaguing you." She paused and gave me another kind smile. "Let me? Please."

"So... you're what—going to drop me off to see my life and then you'll be back around to pick me up again?" I didn't mean to make it sound like we were carpooling but there it was.

"Yes," she answered with that pretty laugh. "There's nothing to worry about, Poppy."

"Alright," I answered with a sigh. "Who-ever you are—the spirit of Christmas, my subconscious, that last glass of eggnog—I guess I can use the help."

Noelle squeezed my hands. "I'm not your subconscious, Poppy." The fluffy white flakes of snow that had been swirling through my kitchen now began to tunnel around us like we were in the middle of a snow globe.

"Okay," I responded, figuring it was best not to argue.

"Remember, Poppy, everything can be changed," Noelle continued. "Nothing is set in stone so whatever you see... you have the power to change it."

"Got it," I answered, as the snow encircling us became thicker, moving faster. I turned to ask Noelle what was happening, but I couldn't see her any longer, yet I could still feel her embrace on my hand as she squeezed one last time before she pulled away. As soon as she did, the kitchen disappeared around me, and I was surrounded by white. The snow was soft as the wind picked me up and carried me back to my bed and I drifted off into sleep.

Somewhere far off, I heard a clock chiming midnight.

Chapter Three

When I finally woke up for real, my head was pounding and I was so tired, my eyes felt gritty.

I lay there for a long moment, hoping the aching in my head would ease off on its own, but no such luck. Advil it was going to need to be.

I had to get up anyway because Finn would be awake soon, and I wanted to get the last few bits of Christmas preparations pulled together before then. If I was quick, I could get coffee and hot chocolate started. Besides, I wanted to see Finn's face when he first came down the stairs and saw the tree all lit up with new presents underneath it.

I just had to find the willpower to get out from under the covers.

Something behind me gave a weird growling roar, and the entire bed trembled. I jumped, my heart in my throat, as I twisted around, and almost catapulted myself onto the floor. My heart was pounding so hard, it felt like it was kicking against the inside of my ribs as I stared down at the other side of the bed.

Marty was lying there, under the covers. One of his feet stuck out the side to dangle down towards the floor. As I watched, his chest rose with a tremendous snore that made the headboard rattle against the wall.

What in the heck was going on? Why was Marty here, in my bed? He hadn't even been over the night before!

Still stunned, I blinked and looked again as I pulled up to stand, all the while trying to calm my frantic heart. It wasn't like it was a monster, it was just Marty but still… it was a little jarring when you went to sleep alone and woke up with… your fiancé.

I swallowed hard at that thought.

As I stood there, studying him, all the

while trying to understand how in the world he was even here, I noticed something. Slight… differences in his face. Yes, this was Marty, but he looked… well, older. For one thing, there were more little lines around his eyes, and at the edges of his mouth. While he'd always been a little salt and pepper around his temples, now the majority of his hair was edging firmly into 'salt' territory. And there was an overall slackness to his skin I didn't recognize. Somehow, Marty had managed to age years in a single night.

I shoved a hand back through my hair, thinking fast.

What was it about the last dream I'd had the night before? I racked my brain, trying to remember what Noelle had said to me. A Christmas wish—it was something like that, I was pretty sure. Something about a glimpse into my own life and I'd been worried she was going to pull a Scrooge move on me?

So… was this the future then? I glanced around the room and noticed there were things that were still the same but other things that were different—for instance, there was an extra chest of drawers that hadn't been there before and Marty's clothes were strewn across the floor on his side of the bed. I glanced over to the open closet and noticed my clothes were stuffed to one side and on the other side? Men's clothes— Marty's clothes.

I swallowed hard as I wondered if I was about to get a visit from the Ghost of Christmas Future who I was pretty sure was supposed to look like something from a Halloween horror movie.

At that concerning thought, I ran my hand through my hair again and this time, it snagged on my fingers, and I swore as I carefully pulled them back. There, on my left ring finger, nestled right up against the beautiful engagement ring Marty had given me, was a wedding band.

I froze, my eyes wide.

Then I reached down and pinched my arm, hard.

It hurt a surprising amount, and I only barely managed to stifle my yelp. I didn't wake up, so this probably wasn't a dream— just like Noelle had said.

So… if it wasn't a dream… just what was it?

A gift. From the Spirit of Christmas.
Oh, brother.

I stared around my bedroom again as I rubbed at the sore spot on my arm. My eyes settled on a picture of Marty and me on the nightstand beside my side of the bed. In it, I was wearing a wedding dress. I couldn't look at it for much longer and instead, my eyes drifted beyond the framed picture to the window. Different curtains.

My gaze drifted over to the chest of drawers where it always stood against the wall as you first walked into my bedroom. Taking a few steps towards it, I noticed a framed picture of a teenaged Finn in some kind of sports uniform, grinning at the camera.

Had Noelle actually done it? Had she transported me into my own future? Was this what she was talking about when she said she had a gift for me? Panic started to cling to me until I remembered how Noelle had said not to worry—that she was simply helping me to understand what decision I should make. I took a deep breath.

Okay, don't panic, I thought. *Everything is going to be okay.*

There was a mirror hanging beside the chest of drawers, and even though half of me dug my heels in, not wanting to see and confirm my own suspicions, I hurried over and took a long, hard look at myself.

Like Marty, I still looked mostly the same as when I'd gone to bed. There were a few more delicate lines decorating the corners of my eyes, and a bit more silver in my blond hair. I had to admit, I was holding up pretty well, however many years this was later.

I shook my head, still reeling with the shock of it all.

This was definitely my future, as far as I could tell. I turned back to look at the bed, where Marty had changed positions and was now snoring away on his side.

In this version of the future, I'd apparently gone through with marrying Marty. So, how far into my future life were we talking?

"I need to find out the date," I whispered to myself as another round of panic overcame me.

Luckily, my nearly falling out of bed, then flailing around, and mumbling to myself hadn't woken Marty up, because I was so not ready for that conversation.

If future me was anything like present me, my phone would be charging downstairs. I could use it to check the date, and get an idea of what in the world was going on in my life and just how far into the future I now was.

With one last glance at Marty who looked like he was doing a great job of impersonating a hibernating bear, I tiptoed towards the door. From the way he was snoring, I probably could have walked a marching band through the middle of the room and still been fine, but I wasn't in the mood to take any chances.

I hurried down the hall towards the stairs, only to skid to a stop as I passed Finn's bedroom.

The door was open, which was strange enough, because Finn never slept with the door open. Was he really up before dawn on Christmas morning? Was it even Christmas morning? Gripping the door frame, I flicked on the light switch and stared.

It was definitely Finn's bedroom, though it was decorated differently—a little bit more mature. It also had a slightly hollow feeling, as if things were missing, making the room feel bigger than I knew it was. The bed was neatly made, but more than that, the way the comforter was creased made it seem as though it hadn't been slept in or disturbed in some time.

My heart gave a tight throb, clenching hard in my chest. My breath came out a little shaky as I exhaled.

Where was Finn? Why wasn't he there? Especially on Christmas? Unless this wasn't Christmas day?

Ugh, I needed to find my phone.

The stairs creaked as I hurried down them. However far into the future I now was, apparently, I still hadn't managed to get all the repairs to the farmhouse done. But that was hardly the most pressing concern I had.

The house was decorated to the rafters with Christmas ornaments and the like, but I barely noticed as I raced through the living room. A tree dominated one corner of the room, so laden with decorations and lights that its branches sagged. There was a miniature Christmas town set up on the mantle of the fireplace that I didn't recognize, but I did note with some relief that there were three stockings hung there. One for me, one for Marty, and one for Finn. Possibly the exact same stockings I'd put up just last night.

Well, however far back 'last night' had really been. Oh, this was going to give me a headache.

Speaking of… the headache I'd awoken with was now nowhere to be found. Apparently waking up years (I thought) into the future was enough to send a headache packing. At least that was one good thing about the shock that was facing me.

But, back to the shock…

Finn's stocking was hanging up. But where was he?

I burst into the kitchen, but it wasn't my phone I saw first, but my laptop set up on the kitchen table. The idle screen was a stock picture of some puppy in a stocking, with a bow around its neck. Immediately my eyes fell on the date that was scrolling across the bottom of the screen, and I had to grab a chair because my knees started to give out on me, wobbling dangerously.

It was Christmas Eve night.

Exactly *five years* into the future.

I stared at that screen for a long time, until a bit of ice fell off the turkey which was defrosting in the sink. The ice made a wet rattle, and the sound pulled me out of my thoughts.

Five years.

That meant Finn would be eighteen, soon to be nineteen. I swallowed hard.

The little sapphire chips in my engagement ring winked in the faint light of the kitchen. The wedding band was a bit plain, but it was a matching white gold, and it fit my finger perfectly.

Married.

I was married to Marty.

Apparently, I had been for years.

My stomach clenched.

I was too tired, and my headache suddenly returned with a vengeance, hurting too much to deal with all of this.

In the course of pulling a pot of coffee together and digging out some Advil from where I still kept it in the top drawer on the left of the stove, I managed to find my phone. The lock screen was a picture of me, Finn, and Marty, all of us smiling with our arms around each other.

I brought my phone back to the table, and after a bracing gulp of too-hot coffee, I opened up the contacts, searching for Finn's name.

The wave of relief I felt when his name appeared right at the top of the most recent messages was so total, that I almost sagged down onto the table. I didn't know what I'd been afraid of (it was one of those thoughts I couldn't even allow myself to think) but now knowing that Finn appeared to be fine, I could breathe again. I hurriedly scrolled up through our latest text messages, guilt nibbling away at the edges of my heart because I felt like I was spying on a private conversation, which I supposed I technically was, but the messages were intended for me. Just not the me that I was or had been, but the me that I would be in five years.

Yikes. That was enough to bring the headache right back.

I promised myself I'd think about the ethics of reading your own, but not yet, texts another time. I didn't have time to feel guilty right now. For now, I had to figure out what in the world was going on.

From what I could piece together, Finn

was currently living away for his first year of university and staying in the dorms. Pride caused a lump to swell up behind my breastbone, and I pressed my hand to my heart as I scrolled further through the conversation.

Finn's exams had run late into the year, but he mentioned looking forward to seeing Marty and me for Christmas. Not far beyond that, I found a few texts where we'd arranged for me to pick him up at the Portland bus terminal on Christmas Eve.

I glanced up at the clock which was still perched over my breakfast table (which was a different table and chairs). I was meant to pick Finn up in a few hours. At the thought that I'd get to see Finn, to assure myself that he was okay, well some of the tension leached out of me, leaving my muscles feeling loose.

It was still a struggle not to call him, so I could hear his voice, and just make sure he was as okay as he appeared to be. But I knew my son well enough to know that no version of him would appreciate a six am wake-up phone call.

I clutched my phone to my chest and smiled.

I could wait a few more hours.

***

The creak of the stairs was my only warning before Marty came lumbering into the kitchen, still looking half asleep. He shuffled towards the coffeepot, but changed directions when his bleary eyes glanced over at me, where I was sitting at the table, drinking my own cup of coffee, and wondering how in the world I was going to get back to my life, five years in the past.

Remembering Noelle's words about not worrying, I pushed the thoughts aside and decided to, instead, trust.

Marty dropped a kiss onto my forehead, pausing long enough to stretch his hands over his head and yawn a, "Good morning, Pops. Merry Christmas Eve."

I noticed that the paunch around his middle was now quite a bit bigger than it had been and I couldn't stifle my amused smile.

"Morning," I managed as I watched him continue to the counter, where it took him a couple seconds to remember where I kept the mugs and once he did, he returned to the coffeepot.

I had to fight back a smile. I always knew Marty was the furthest thing from a morning person. Between his freelance graphic design business, and his ghost busting business, he was a lot more likely to see dawn from the other side than be up at six am. But that didn't make his slow, sleepy shuffle any less entertaining.

Marty turned away from the counter, squinting at me. He lifted the coffeepot up, and kind of waggled it at me. At first, I thought he'd given up on trying to pour it into a mug and was just going straight for the source, but I finally clued in that he was asking me if I wanted more.

"No, thank you." I showed him the mostly full cup in my hands. "I've still got some."

With another sleepy little mumble, Marty went about fixing his own cup.

I cradled my mug between my hands, letting the heat of it soak into my fingers. It was nice, being here with Marty just like usual, while everything outside was dark, soft, and quiet.

If I was being honest though, while I was

always happy to see Marty, everything felt… comfortable. Like this was the way we woke up each and every morning—like I would watch Marty struggle into the kitchen, stretch and stifle a yawn with his hair standing straight on end and sleep still gunked into the corners of his eyes. I glanced down at the faded pajamas I was wearing and couldn't help but feel that just like my worn-out pjs, we'd worn ourselves into a familiar groove, and while it felt nice and comfy… it also seemed to be missing something.

While Roy, my ex-boyfriend, and I hadn't worked out, on account of him having a soulmate in Fifi, there had always been passion in our relationship. Excitement. I'd always been able to feel the prickle of awareness whenever we were physically near each other.

Or Andre…

But that was a name and a subject I wasn't going to touch.

I managed to work up a smile as Marty plunked himself down into the chair opposite me, cradling his coffee like it was a lifeline. He couldn't seem to manage to keep his eyes open until after the first few swallows from his mug.

"You awake?" I teased, and Marty gave me a sleepy smile.

"Almost." He yawned. "You're picking Finn up from the bus station, right?" he asked. I nodded and then he nodded. "I can finish up the last of the wrapping while you're out."

Warm fondness filled me as I watched Marty finish his cup of coffee and then he yawned once more before he appeared to be even remotely awake.

"Thanks, McFly," I said on a laugh.

That made him blink and there was a surprised expression on his face when he looked over at me. "You haven't called me that in a while," he said with a lopsided, goofy smile. "Like… in years."

I shrugged, lifting my mug up for a hasty swallow of coffee, hoping it hid my slip-up. "I'm feeling nostalgic," I muttered against the rim.

Normally, I loved the quiet mornings. Just me and my coffee, watching the sun rise through my kitchen window as I thought about getting Finn up and ready for school.

But with Marty here, my mind was racing. I just didn't know what to say that wouldn't come off as odd, given the fact that I was still five years in the past and he... wasn't.

Anxiety crawled up my spine. The quiet between us wasn't companionable. It felt suffocating. Suddenly, the cozy familiar kitchen felt a little claustrophobic. The rings on my left hand suddenly weighed twenty pounds and it was all I could do to remain sitting. I was just too worried I might say the wrong thing, or do something Marty would consider strange. My nerves were pulled tight and humming like violin strings and I put my mug down on the table a little too hard.

"So," I started. "I was thinking of going into town to pick up a couple last minute things before I head to Portland to get Finn. Do you, uh, need anything?"

Marty squinted at me, and a little prickle ran down my spine. Did he suspect something was off? Was this not how future Poppy acted? Was I screwing this whole thing up?

But no, it was just Marty's morning brain taking a minute to boot up.

"Mmm, don't think so." He blinked, taking another long sip of his coffee. "I didn't have any plans today, other than puttering around and helping you with whatever you need."

"Oh, okay."

Shoving away from the table, I carried my mug over to the sink, suddenly eager to get out of the kitchen. "Okay, I'm going to go take a shower, then." At least I could probably draw out getting ready until the stores were soon to open, though I felt a little guilty leaving Marty just sitting there by himself.

But he didn't seem to mind. He just smiled as a little expression of mischief crossed his face. "You want me to join you?"

At the thought of him joining me in the shower, I swallowed hard. "Um, no, I'm feeling a little... *hurried* this morning."

He nodded and looked a little disappointed, even as I was relieved. "Okay, Pops."

It took some effort, but I managed to keep my steps even and not look like I was fleeing the room.

Chapter Four

Haven Hollow was beautiful under a blanket of freshly fallen snow.

Everything looked a little too perfect, like a Christmas card. I couldn't help but wonder if some of the supernaturals had banded together to make the town look so picturesque for the holiday tourists. Maybe things with the Winter Court of Faeries had calmed down enough that we could have a peaceful Christmas, again. Wars of succession had a way of complicating the holidays.

The town Council had gone all out with their decorating. The entire downtown was done up with pretty garlands of evergreen boughs decorating all the telephone poles, and wreaths on the street lights. Every storefront featured painted windows with Christmassy scenes and all the trees were wound up in white fairy lights.

There was a cluster of white wicker reindeer on the lawn outside Stomper's Creamery, lit up from beneath with a spotlight. Sweeter Haunt's front window was filled with fake snow and little lights to better show off the candy canes, peanut brittle, marshmallow Santas, and hot cocoa bombs that were on display there. Just walking past it had my mouth watering.

Up the street, I could see the Half-Moon Bar and Grill, still closed this early in the day, but someone had gone to a lot of effort to flock the windows with fake snow, so they looked like something from Santa's workshop.

Even Wanda's Witchery was done up for the holidays. Though witches actually celebrated Yule this time of year and weren't necessarily big on Christmas, Wanda had always had a good instinct for what would draw customers into her store, and it had only gotten better once her cousin, Maverick, had started working for her. Maverick might have been a cantankerous grouch, but he was actually more pleasant to customers than Wanda was, herself.

I strolled up the sidewalk, my hands in my pockets, and looked in through the windows at the mannequins on display there, each of them wearing an absolutely gorgeous holiday dress. Office parties were big business, especially when the clothing was enchanted for poise and confidence, and maybe even impressing someone enough to get a promotion out of the deal.

My eyes drifted, and I realized with a little surprise that Wanda's shop had actually expanded into the space next door, where a stationery store had been before. I was beyond happy to know that Wanda was doing so well in the future that she was able to expand her shop. The window display in what was once the stationery store was now taken up with beautiful and sexy satin pajamas, which were, according to the sign, guaranteed to give the wearer the best night's sleep.

That made me think of my own restless night's sleep, and my stomach gave a little unpleasant twist. I had to turn away sharply at the memory of the dream in which Marty had accused me of not being in love with him.

From what I could tell, it wasn't like marrying Marty had ended up... *bad* necessarily. That morning was a perfect example of how things were cozy and comfortable between us—just like I was used to. There had been a definite feeling of peaceful domesticity, of easy familiarity. Marty was one of my favorite people and being able to spend the rest of my life with him... well, it would be nice.

It *was* nice. I'd just witnessed that first-hand.

Right?

Yes, but...

Something was missing.

Something was always missing.

Searching for a distraction, I let myself look over across the street to where my own store stood proudly. I walked across the brick expanse, eager to see if anything had changed inside Poppy's Potions.

The outside of my store was all done up for Christmas, with a display of delicate glass bottles and an array of candles already anointed and ready to be lit. There were garlands hung around the edges of the window, with little glass ornaments hanging from the evergreen boughs, and I made a little sound of excitement at how pretty it all was.

My store hadn't expanded like Wanda's, but then, potions took up a heck of a lot less room than gowns, purses and shoes. I was eager to see any changes made to the inside of the shop, so I fumbled my keys out of my pocket and let myself in. A little gasp escaped me as I flicked on the overhead lights and stared at all the glittering displays.

All my antique, heavy wooden cabinets were still there, which was good because I loved how they made the store look like an old-time apothecary shop. But glass shelves had been interspersed between them, along with dark wood racks towards the back of the store. The glass shelves had beautiful little fairy lights draped over them, shining straight through and making everything look like it had been carved out of gleaming ice.

I wandered the aisles, running my fingers along a shelf here, examining a potion bottle there, and taking notes about the ideas that I absolutely loved so I could work them into my own plans as soon as possible. Was that cheating? Maybe. But some of them were just too good to pass up.

I loved being inside my shop. There was something about all the gleaming dark wood, and the pretty glass, as well as the scents of almond oil and citrus and clove that just helped to melt the tension from my shoulders.

One thing I noticed though, after my second spin through the rows of shelves, was the change in my stock. Well, not *change* exactly. More like a whole line of potions was decidedly missing. While there were still tons of different types of potions, dreamcatchers and anointed candles, and even a couple examples of wax melts that were infused, some of my more popular recipes seemed to be missing.

I never stocked anything dangerous, or illicit like hexing type potions. That just wasn't my style—not the sort of mojo I wanted to put out into the world. So it wasn't the lack of dark potions that had caught my attention. More, it was the lack of love-related potions and the sexier side of the love potions like lust potions that were causing me to do a double-take.

I'd always carried a few harmless… *adult* potions. Nothing dirty, no matter how many times Astrid might have accused me (just to get a rise out of me). But potions like *Love's Goddess*, or *Come to Me* oil or *Aura of Venus*, all of which could be used to attract male attention. Some were excellent as massage oils with an intimate partner. And some could be used to, ah, help warm the ol' engine up, so to say. The point was, I used to have a discrete little shelf section towards the back of the store for people who were looking to spice things up in the bedroom or to get the attention of that cute co-worker they'd been eyeing.

But that section and those potions were now gone. In fact, as I moved around the future version of my store, I couldn't find a single potion that had anything to do with love, lust, or really any strong emotion at all. Could it be that I was just sold out? But as soon as that thought crossed my mind, I immediately discarded it. It didn't seem possible to have sold out of *every one* of them. Maybe I just didn't carry them any longer?

That seemed kind of short sighted though. Love and lust potions were some of my biggest sellers.

So, why had I stopped carrying love potions?

A little nagging feeling of something being off squirmed through me and even though I tried to shake the feeling away, it wouldn't go.

Why had I stopped carrying love potions?!

Unless a lot of things had changed in just five years, I still had one place to check for the answer.

My own notes.

Potion making could be an intensely personal thing. Mostly, I followed the same recipes as my mother and her mother before her, but sometimes I made little adjustments, here and there, following my own instincts regarding what felt right to me. And I tended to keep a lot of notes of my experiments: notes on what worked, what didn't, and what I thought might have gone wrong if something wasn't successful. The notes helped me hone my craft, and I was fairly sure I hadn't stopped writing them because they'd been a huge part of my potion making all along.

It took a bit of searching, but eventually I found the little leather-bound notebook tucked under the drawer in the antique cash register. Flipping through it took some work. Quite a few things had changed in five years, after all, and one of them seemed to be how I sorted my note taking. I had to turn back quite a few pages to find the answer to my question. And when I did, my heart sank.

From what I read in my notes, it seemed I hadn't been able to brew any strong love or lust-based potions for the past three years. Each time I tried, the magic just didn't seem to want to stick.

Today I tried to brew Charlotte's Web, I read from my notes in an entry dated two years ago. *But the potion just sort of fizzled when I joined the ingredients, leaving a limp gray mess that did nothing and smelled even worse.*

That was strange.

More than strange, actually. It was unnerving because *Charlotte's Web* was one of my easiest love potions to brew and one of my biggest sellers.

Oh, sure, I'd botched potions before. I'd let myself get distracted, or maybe I'd get the ratio of my ingredients off. It happened, especially when I was first learning. And then again after I'd joined Wanda's coven and my magic got pretty funky for a bit. I guessed that was what happened when you melded with a group of witches, some of them Blood Witches, infected with vampire blood. Most recently, I was still trying to figure out where they ended and I began.

At least Wanda's inability to brew a potion hadn't infected me. I'd never made anything explode, so there was that. But I'd also never just had potions stop working for me.

I slipped the notebook back into its hiding place and shivered, feeling suddenly chilled in spite of the warmth of the store. There was just this uneasiness building inside me, making my stomach churn.

I suddenly needed some fresh air, so I left the sign turned to closed and locked the store back up. It was for the best, anyway. What if someone came in who'd ordered something and I didn't know what in the world they were talking about? It would seem like I'd lost my mind. Besides, I would need to leave for Portland in a little bit to pick up Finn. Future me would just have to deal with the loss of revenue of last-minute potion shoppers.

And on that thought, I had another one—what about Future Me? Was I going to walk into myself five years from now? And if that happened, would the world cease to be or something? The more I thought about it though, the more I didn't think it was possible. It wasn't like I'd arrived five years in the future, looking like Poppy from five years in the past. As far as I could tell, I was Poppy five years from now—I just had no memory of the years that had gone by.

I almost crossed the street to go back to Wanda's shop. My witch BFF always had a way of putting things into perspective for me, usually with a near lethal dose of sarcasm, true, but I appreciated her brutal honesty.

Then I remembered, Wanda wouldn't be in her store, not while the sun was up, at least. I was assuming that, five years down the road, she'd still be pretending to have been turned into a vampire by Lorcan. That was how they'd managed to get the covens and the vampires off their backs about Wanda being a Blood Witch. I didn't see that changing anytime soon, and that had to mean she'd still kept up her nocturnal life-style.

So, really, there was no one I could talk to. It was a little disappointing, but at least the town looked beautiful in all its holiday finery. As I stood there, a gentle snow started, glittering flakes falling from the pewter clouds like something out of a fairy tale. The nice kind of fairy tale, for children, at least. But as far as the Fae went, I didn't trust them as far as I could throw them.

As I walked back down Main Street, looking at the lights and the trees and the red ribbon wrapped lamppost that looked like a candy cane, with the carols trickling through the air each time a door opened, I just couldn't seem to enjoy it. Christmas was one of my favorite times of year, and yet I couldn't seem to get into the spirit of things at all. There was this pit inside my stomach, an aching kind of hollowness, and I just couldn't seem to shake it.

The door to the Half-Moon opened as I

was walking up the street, and Fifi stepped out into the snow, looking like a supermodel doing a winter fashion shoot. Fifi was one of the nicest people I knew. She might have been a terrible demon, but she was a great real estate agent, and she was a great friend.

As a lust demon, it was hard for Fifi to ever look bad. She was perfectly proportioned, with glittering silver hair down to her tailbone, and a face that made people do a double take. I'd seen it happen before. One poor guy almost fell down the stairs once. But that morning, with the snow falling around her, and a smile on her ethereal face, Fifi was practically glowing.

The reason for her extra sparkle stepped out the door behind her, bending down from his towering height to press a kiss to her lips.

Roy, my ex-boyfriend, raised his head, but stayed hunched over so he could say something to Fifi in that low, growling voice of his that made her giggle and brought a pretty flush to her cheeks.

You might have thought it was the sight of my ex so obviously in love with another woman that was the cause for the breath catching in my throat. Roy and I had been good together, true. He was amazing. But I'd broken up with him once I realized he and Fifi were soulmates. Literally. A witch had pulled me aside to warn me that Roy was bound by fate to another woman and that didn't seem to be good for the longevity of our own relationship.

I couldn't compete with that. Heck, I didn't *want* to compete with that. Soulmates were such a rare and precious thing, to find your person, the other half of your soul. Who would ever want to get in the middle of that?

So, no, it wasn't the way the two of them curved in towards each other that had my hand flying up to press over my heart, though it did give a little twinge. It was the little blanket wrapped bundle that Roy had tucked into the crook of his arm, a thatch of silvery blond hair poking up at the top, that had me fighting back a squeal.

Roy passed the baby carefully to Fifi, his big hands so gentle, and she took the little bundle with a practiced movement, already rocking slightly from side to side. She said something back to him and then turned towards the SUV parked at the curb. Together, they carefully got the baby settled into a car seat, and with another kiss, Fifi got in the driver's side and pulled away, while Roy waved before heading back into the Half-Moon.

I could have gone over and said Merry Christmas, and taken a look at the baby. But somehow, I just couldn't make myself take the steps. Neither of them had noticed me, and it wasn't until the door swung shut behind Roy that I finally managed to take a gasping breath.

I stood there for a long moment, with the snow falling all around me, not understanding why I felt like I was missing something. The lights were beautiful, and the smell of shortbread dancing on the air was its own kind of magical. The town was practically alive with the magic of Christmas and my friends appeared to be so, so happy.

So why wasn't I?

Chapter Five

I wandered through the town, past all the cheerfully decorated shops.

But my own mood hung over me like a soggy blanket, making it hard for me to appreciate the charm of Haven Hollow at Christmas time. A car drove by, too close to the curb, and splattered gray slush across the pristine snow ahead of me.

I tried not to take it as a sign.

Before I could sink too far into the doldrums, my phone chirped, alerting me to a text message. There weren't a lot of people out and about at this hour, but I stepped to the side as I fished my cell out of my pocket so as not to block the sidewalk.

The message was from Marty.

Pops, it read. *I hope you're having a good wander. Could pick up eggs before you head home? I thought I'd make my world-famous nog.*

As someone who'd experienced Marty's eggnog before, I wasn't sure how world-famous it was. But he loved making it, and it was drinkable, so I kept my mouth shut about the slightly too thick texture and the cloying sweetness that was a little off-putting.

I fired off a quick: *Of course, see you soon.*

Then I hit 'send'.

Curiosity gripped me, and I ended up leaning back against the gritty brick wall of a store front so I could scroll up through my past text conversations with Marty. It was odd, and a little uncomfortable, reading things that were obviously from me, but that I hadn't written. Or, at least, that I hadn't written yet?

It was all very confusing to think about.

The further back I read, the lower my mood sank. It wasn't that there was anything wrong with our conversation—no arguments or mean words. Actually, it was the opposite —we were nothing but cheerful and nice, but the conversations between us could very easily have been mistaken for that between roommates, not a married couple. They were all friendly texts, affectionate even, but there was nothing spicy about them—nothing that hinted at both people being irrefutably *in love* with one another.

Not one of those messages made my heart race.

Almost against my will, the memory of Roy and Fifi in front of the Half-Moon popped into my head. The way they'd leaned into each other. The way Roy had curved his big body down to accommodate Fifi's smaller stature. The way she'd reached out idly to touch his chest, his shoulder, his arm, as though she couldn't bear for even a few inches to separate them. The way they'd whispered to each other, smiling, both of them in their own little world right there on the street.

I shoved my phone back into my pocket and turned to head back to where I'd parked the Jeep (which was the same as the one I had five years ago only decided more broken in). I couldn't have even explained why to myself, but hot tears were pressing against the corners of my eyes, and my throat was thick when I swallowed.

It was silly.

I didn't know why I was upset.

But here I was, five years into the future, walking down Main Street with tears in my eyes.

The town felt like it was closing in on me a little, almost suffocating me which made no sense at all. With a firm resolution, I decided the best thing to do was just to head out to Portland and wait for Finn to arrive. It was still hours before I needed to pick him up, but at least Portland would be a change of scenery. Between my store, and Finn, and the general mayhem of Haven Hollow, I didn't get into Portland very often. It would be nice to see it all done up for the holidays.

The drive was pretty uneventful. I sang along to the Christmas carols on the radio even though I couldn't say my heart was really in it. All the while, I tried to keep my thoughts from wandering back to that text conversation with Marty and how completely lackluster it had been.

Instead, I focused on the fact that I was going to see Finn. Five years wasn't a big deal between forty-five and fifty, but it was an enormous difference between thirteen and eighteen. Finn was an adult now, all grown up and away at school. And that thought hollowed out the inside of my stomach even more than it already was.

Even so, I couldn't wait to get a look at him, to see the type of man my son would grow up to become. The thought was a little bittersweet. It already felt like Finn was growing up way, way too fast—like just yesterday I was holding his little chubby toddler hand to cross the street.

I wondered if he'd kept up with his magic studies. Thirteen-year-old Finn was completely determined to learn as much about becoming a Magician as possible. He was already an adept healer, and he'd learned several impressive magic tricks, including dream walking, which apparently was a big deal. I hadn't been thrilled that he was using his dreams to effectively sneak out and learn magic behind my back, especially when I didn't know what the risks were. Now I wanted to be able to console myself that all that worrying was for nothing.

Hopefully.

My rings suddenly felt cold on my finger. I adjusted the heater vent and did my best to ignore the pins and needles that seemed to be emanating from the gold band and down my ring finger, into my hand, and now up my arm.

Hmm, that was strange.

I forced my thoughts back to Finn as I wondered if this five years in the future version of him would have lost interest in becoming a Magician. Magic was fascinating to a child, the idea of having powers and fighting back the darkness. But teenagers, their priorities shifted. Maybe Finn had put away his tricks when he'd gone off to college.

Why did I feel hopeful about that?

I shifted in my seat, uncomfortable but not sure why. So, I turned up the radio and sang along to the catchy lyrics of 'Jingle Bell Rock'.

Until that weird icy feeling started up in my ring finger again and sighing with defeat, I removed both rings and placed them in the center consul of the Jeep. Strangely, as soon as I took the rings off, that icy feeling stopped.

***

Portland was a big city, the largest in the state, and while it didn't have the same small-town charm that Haven Hollow played up, it was still beautiful under a blanket of snow. The bridge I'd driven over to get into the city had been all strung up with lights, and while it was pretty during the day, it must have looked absolutely magical at night. The river cut a gleaming blue ribbon through the city, sparkling under the soft winter sun.

Now no longer in Haven Hollow, I felt like I could finally take a full breath, no longer feeling like the buildings were folding in around me.

Yes, it was a good idea to leave early and spend some time in Portland. I hadn't been here very many times, so I still felt like a tourist as I peeked at this and got awed by that. There was just so much to take in, so many people zooming here and there as they did their last-minute Christmas shopping. I decided to park the Jeep near the bus station and then figured I had some time to go take a little walk through the downtown area.

After parking, I walked past a grocery store and almost got run over in the lot by a little old lady with a cart full of what looked like pumpkin pies. She gave me an embarrassed laugh and I responded with the same as a bakery display caught my eye. Turning to look through the flocked window at the lovely boxes of cakes and cookies, my stomach growled. The fruit cake looked like something made of stained glass, shimmering under the lights. Ginger snaps were dusted in sugar, and I could almost feel the crispness of them under my teeth. But what snagged my attention was a gorgeous tray of candy cane shortbread cookies. They just looked so buttery and delicious.

Marty had one heck of a sweet tooth, so I knew he'd appreciate some cookies and more specifically, *those* cookies. The little red and green candy cane bits sticking out of the shortbread reminded me of the candy cane Noelle had left on the counter at my store. I took the thought of Noelle as a sign and slipped through the foggy bakery door.

As soon as I stepped inside, the smell of warm baking bread flooded my nose, and I tipped my head back to inhale greedily. I looked at a few more things before I solidified my decision to get the shortbread and headed to the checkout line. As I waited in line, I looked over the glass display counter, seeing if there was anything else there that Finn and Marty might like. Maybe some freshly baked croissants for breakfast, or some challah to make the perfect French Toast. It was warm and cozy inside, the welcoming smell of good things baking wrapping around my shoulders like a hug.

"Poppy?" A familiar man's voice spoke up behind me. "Is that you?"

I jolted, surprised out of my browsing. I really hadn't expected to bump into anyone I knew in Portland which wasn't exactly close to Haven Hollow.

I turned on my heel and came face to face with... Andre.

I just stood there and stared, too surprised to react at first.

Andre looked exactly the same as I remembered him.

There might have been a few more lines on his brow, and a bit of silver in his dark hair, but he still looked… well, he still looked just as handsome as he always had. He was still just as tall, and trim under his dark wool pea coat. And he still seemed to favor the same dark colors that contrasted so perfectly with his light skin and blue eyes. There was a scarf wrapped around his neck, done in a pulled-through loop the British seemed to favor. His broad shoulders were dusted with the snow from outside, and though he was smiling and obviously pleased to see me, there was something about the way his brows had pinched together that made me think he seemed a little sad, too.

But that was silly. Why should Andre be sad to see me? I shook the ridiculous notion off and, instead, tried to remember my manners. But in order to remember my manners, I first needed to remember how to form words—a lesson that didn't seem to be coming well.

"Oh, my, um…" I stammered before letting out a strange little laugh as my cheeks colored with heat. "Andre…"

And even though I was hoping it wouldn't be, *it* was still there—that intense feeling of familiarity. That same magnetic pull. As if every part of me just wanted to take that step forward, throw my arms around him and never let go.

But that was just Poppy from five years before talking—I was more than sure that five years into the future, I wouldn't still feel this way. Yet, it was five years into the future…

Anyway… I was still just standing there, staring up at this incredibly handsome man who was still… staring down at me. It seemed neither one of us could find our tongues.

"Yes, it's… me," he said softly.

"I… ha! I'm surprised to see you," I managed, sounding like a complete and total idiot. It was embarrassing enough to bring another flush to my face, but I couldn't keep myself from smiling widely at Andre. In spite of the strange things he made me feel, I was very happy to see him.

"Not as surprised as I am to see you, I can assure you," he answered in that posh accent of his that had haunted me ever since I'd first met him.

"What... what are you doing here?"

He motioned to the freshly made loaf of bread in his arms. "Toast for Boxing Day," he answered on a wide grin. "You?"

I motioned to the shortbread cookies nestled in my hand. "Holiday cookies."

"You came all the way to Portland to pick up cookies?" he asked with a laugh.

"Oh, no," I answered, flushing all the way from my toes to the crown of my head. "I, uh... " I beamed at him as I wrestled with my heart to stop beating so damned hard. "How, um, how... are you?"

"I'm very well, thank you," he said and then that smile was in full effect and I felt suddenly weak in my knees. "So if you aren't in Portland for the shortbread cookies?"

"Oh," I started, feeling my eyebrows reaching for the ceiling. "I, um, I'm here to get Finn, actually. He's away at college and he's coming back to Haven Hollow for Christmas."

"You're picking him up from the bus station?"

I nodded. "Yes, but he's not due to arrive for a couple of hours."

"How fortuitous," Andre answered with a quick nod.

"Fortuitous?" I repeated, like I'd never heard the word before.

He nodded again. "Would you like to grab a table—to catch up for a bit?"

That had to mean we hadn't seen each other in a while, then? As far as I knew, we hadn't seen one another for the last five years, but it wasn't like I could just come right out and ask him as much. My spirits dimmed for some reason, but I made sure to keep the expression off my face as I agreed.

We grabbed a coffee (which Andre insisted on paying for), and I tucked my package of shortbread onto the window ledge next to our table as we sat down, my heart still riding into my throat. God, there was just something about this man—there always had been and I imagined there always would be.

I shrugged out of my coat, trying to keep my elbows tucked in so as not to bump anyone walking past.

"Poppy Morton," Andre said as soon as

we were both seated across from one another. His grin was broad and his eyes shone with obvious happiness. "You look very well."

"Thank you," I managed. "As do you."

"I'm dying to know: how have you been?"

In my time, Andre was planning to relocate to Haven Hollow after spending most of his life as a traveling performer, going from place to place to spread magic and help people. Portland wasn't terribly far from the Hollow, but it was still strange to bump into him here. Of course, there had been that conversation we'd had when Andre had said he had to return to Portland on business, so maybe he'd just never left? Or he'd left Portland and returned? Either way, it seemed he'd left Haven Hollow for good. And that was a thought that saddened me.

"I've... I've been well," I started, struggling with whether or not I should tell him the truth—that I wasn't sure if I was just dreaming this whole thing or if Christmas magic had really managed to send me forward into the future. But that was such a huge topic, and I was suddenly too exhausted to even think about bringing it up. Instead, I just wanted to focus on my handsome... *friend* and find out what had kept him occupied all these years.

No matter what was going on in my head, it really was wonderful to see him.

Andre set his mug back on the little table and rested his forearms on the edge. He still wore a long-sleeved turtleneck sweater, to hide the black tattooed numbers that appeared on his skin with each new trick he learned. And from what I'd been able to tell, Andre had a lot of them. That had sure freaked me out, when black lines started etching themselves onto Finn's skin like tattoos from the inside out.

"And you?" I asked, hoping my smile wasn't shaking like the rest of me. I was nervous, though I couldn't quite say why. "What are you doing in Portland?"

"Oh, I live here," he answered with a quick shrug.

"You live here?" I repeated, clearly surprised. "You, the *traveling* Magician—emphasis on the word 'traveling'?"

He chuckled at that and then glanced down into his cup of steaming coffee. "Yes,

I guess you could say I finally put down roots."

I couldn't say why that information bothered me but it did. "Oh."

He looked up at me and there was something in his eyes—it was the same thing that had always been in his eyes and I still struggled to identify it. "I opened up a magic shop here, a few years back."

"You did?"

He nodded. "I did and I'm pleased to say it's doing quite well."

My heart sank, but I kept my smile in place, even as I asked myself why Andre putting down roots in Portland bothered me so much. I just couldn't understand why here and not Haven Hollow? What had made him leave the Hollow for Portland? It seemed kind of an odd choice him settling here, especially when Haven Hollow was an ideal place for a magic store. Not only that, but we didn't have a magic shop.

He took another sip of coffee, his eyes searching my face. "What about you? Where are you living now?"

"Oh, I'm still in Haven Hollow," I answered quickly.

"Still running the potion shop?"

I nodded. "The shop is doing really well." At least, I assumed it was. It had looked fairly prosperous even if I was still worried about the fact that I'd stopped being able to brew some of my famous recipes.

"And you said Finn is coming home from university for Christmas?"

I nodded. "I'm just in town to pick him up."

That got a more genuine smile out of Andre, the corners of his eyes crinkling up. "That's wonderful. He comes to visit me sometimes."

"He does?" I asked, the shock and surprise dripping into my tone.

"Yes," Andre nodded and his smile seemed sad again. "Mostly when dream walking. We haven't really spoken lately, though—I suppose he's just busy with his studies. I'm glad to know he's doing well— he's such a talented and exceptional young man."

That made me falter, and I grabbed my coffee to buy myself time to respond.

Andre hadn't heard from Finn? What did that mean? Had Finn given up on being a

Magician? Hmm, it didn't seem so—not if Finn was visiting Andre in his dreams. Once upon a time, Andre had volunteered to be Finn's teacher, and he'd been planning to move to Haven Hollow to do it. Well, before he'd been called back to Portland. So, what could have changed that would make them only speak occasionally now? Surely Finn couldn't have mastered every trick in the Magician's Grimoire (known as 'Ouire') in just a couple of years?

My son might be something of a magical prodigy, but no one was *that* good. At least, I didn't think they were.

How on earth was I going to ask Andre about it though? Or Finn, for that matter?

Finally, after a few more minutes of painfully light small talk, I just bit the bullet and decided to start in on the heavier subjects.

"So," I started, as casually as I could. "What made you decide to move to Portland? You seemed so ready to settle in Haven Hollow."

Andre, who had just been about to take a sip of his coffee, set his mug down instead. There was a pause so long and so awkward that I desperately wished I'd just minded my own business. Andre's gaze fell to the white tablecloth, and he seemed almost anxious as he traced the floral embroidery with his index finger.

Finally, he looked up at me and gave me an apologetic smile. "Well." He cleared his throat, an expression passing over his face that I would have almost called 'rueful'. "I suppose it was... shortly after you'd gotten engaged to Marty."

"Oh?" I started, swallowing hard as my heart started to pound in earnest again.

He nodded. "I just couldn't seem to bear to be in the Hollow, after that."

I stared at him in surprise, not sure what to say. Something inside my chest gave a painful twist as I wondered if Andre's words meant what I thought they'd meant. I didn't know what kind of expression I was making, but it must have been something, because Andre made a little aborted reach for my hand.

"I'm sorry," he said quietly. "I don't want to upset you."

"No," I answered immediately and glanced down as I watched myself reach for him. I wrapped my fingers around his hand and was surprised by the warmth of him. "You haven't upset me."

He nodded and then breathed in deeply as he shook his head. "It was my own fault, really."

I looked up at him, painfully aware of how he turned his hand around and closed his fingers around mine. "What was your fault?"

"Never having the courage to speak up. Never having the courage to tell you how I felt," he answered and there was a fire in his eyes and his words. "It's one of those things I most regret, Poppy."

I couldn't have spoken even if I'd known what to say. My throat felt too tight, like all my emotions had gotten tangled up in a messy knot.

Andre smiled, but it was sad, almost wistful.

"I... I don't know what to say," I managed finally, shaking my head as I breathed in deeply and told myself not to cry, even as I could feel the tears threatening. "I always thought... the feelings I had... that *I* was the only one feeling them."

Andre immediately shook his head then, and an almost angry smile overtook his mouth. "No, you weren't the only one." He looked at me and sighed. "Certainly not." Then he took a deep breath. "I knew... I always knew but the truth... well, I suppose it frightened me."

"You knew... what?"

"*Who* you were," he answered on a laugh.

"Who I was?" I was confused.

He nodded and then took another deep breath, as if he were refueling his courage. "From the moment I first walked up to you, when you were about to drop all your potions and I froze them in the air, only to drop them for you," he started on a laugh and I joined in as I remembered the moment. "From the exact second I laid eyes on you, Poppy, I felt... this... *connection*. I can't rightly explain it, but it feels as if I've known you forever."

"I always felt that too."

"Even beyond this life," he continued, sighing again. "As if it was my soul that recognized yours." Then he shook his head and chuckled. "I know this sounds utterly bonkers."

"No," I insisted as I squeezed his hand even harder than he was squeezing mine. "It doesn't. Because I know exactly what you're talking about."

He nodded and then glanced down at our hands as if he was only now noticing them. "I just couldn't stay in Haven Hollow when I realized you were meant to marry someone else," he continued, his voice deep and small. He inhaled deeply and shook his head as his eyes met mine again. His appeared even sadder than they had before. "I'm sorry. I'm not trying to upset you…" he continued as he, no doubt, saw the sheen of tears reflecting in my eyes. "I just… perhaps I just needed to get this off my chest. Even if it is too late." He smiled at me then and I was sure the smile I gave him in return was just as sad. "I wish I had told you how I felt all those years ago."

I managed to force my voice out past the tightness of my throat. It came out thin and a little wobbly. "I wish you had, too."

Then, in a motion that seemed completely out of sync, he pushed aside his half-finished coffee, clearing his throat as he stood up from the table. It was almost as if the chair or my hand had bitten him. He gave me a strange expression before checking the clock on the wall. "I've kept you long enough, Poppy," he said with a laugh that I was more than sure he couldn't feel. "I know you have to get to the station. I do hope you will give my best to Finn?"

"Yes, yes of course," I answered as I glanced up at the clock and was amazed to see that an hour had gone by. It had felt more like fifteen minutes. I stood as well and watched Andre pause after he'd pulled his coat and scarf back on, his hands tucked into his pockets.

"I am so pleased I was able to run into you today, Poppy."

I felt like I was going to lose the battle with my tears and just managed to nod as I said, "Me too."

"Well, goodbye, Poppy. It was really lovely to see you." He managed a small smile, just a slight curve at the corners of his lips. "And Happy Christmas."

Before I could come up with any kind of reply, he was gone.

Chapter Six

I sat at the bakery table for a long time after Andre left.

My coffee was cold as people came and went, laughing, chatting, and stomping their feet against the cold outside.

I barely noticed them.

Instead, I stared at my left hand, at the place where my wedding rings were supposed to be. Strangely, ever since I'd taken them off, that feeling of frosty coldness had disappeared. And even more strangely, Andre hadn't remarked about their absence—especially when he'd been holding that hand so he must have noticed...

He was probably just too polite to comment.

Thoughts about my rings and Andre not noticing them then led to thoughts about Marty and our marriage and I could feel that cloud of doubt pressing down on me—just the same as it had been from the moment Marty had popped the question at my Thanksgiving table.

I didn't know what to do.

I loved Marty; I knew I did.

But I also knew I wasn't *in* love with him.

And with this little trip into the future, it was pretty apparent those feelings or lack thereof wouldn't change. Oh, sure, we were comfortable together, we always had been. And it appeared that we'd settled in together like a house sinking into its foundation.

But there was no spark, no romance.

We might be partners and the best of friends, but we didn't *feel* like a couple.

Marty was definitely the safe choice. The life I saw laid out in front of me was a good one, even. Companionable. Comfortable. Fun. That was more than a lot of people had. But, I wondered as I stared unhappily down at the table, was I content with that? Was companionable, comfortable, and fun… was that enough for me?

Thinking back to the love potions in my store, I had a sneaking suspicion regarding why future me was having such a hard time brewing them. Love and intimacy potions required passion, and you couldn't put into magic what you, yourself, didn't feel. That could only mean one thing—that marrying Marty would equate to a lack of passion—a lack of desire in my life. Did I want to sign up for that?

When Andre had blown into Haven Hollow, he'd seemed like an impossible dream. A Magician who traveled the country, helping people, saving them really, bringing hope to the hopeless. It was all very exciting, but I wasn't twenty. I was a forty-something mom, and Finn and I were settled in Haven Hollow—we were happy there, building a life together. And even if Andre did have feelings for me, he still wasn't a safe bet—he didn't even have a solid home, for Pete's sake!

But I still couldn't help the feelings I had for him.

It was somehow better and worse at the same time, knowing that he'd always felt the same way.

And while it certainly seemed like things might have worked out differently, if Andre and I had ever actually had a conversation about how we felt about each other, there was still no guarantee that such a conversation would have actually changed anything. Even if we'd both confessed what was truly in our hearts, there was no assurance that we'd have ended up together. Or that Andre wouldn't have packed up and left the Hollow for whatever reason.

Fate was funny like that. Fickle. You might see your path ahead, and think you were headed down a certain road, only to end up in a totally different place, all the while wondering—how in the world did I end up here?

All told, Marty was always the safer choice. He was *still* the safer choice.

We'd built a home together, shared our lives and, from what I could tell, we were happy or happy *enough*.

Was that what I wanted, though? Was 'happy enough' going to sustain me for the rest of my life?

The thought kept nagging at me, nipping at my heels like a badly trained dog. I finally grabbed my coat and left that bakery in the center of downtown Portland, completely forgetting my cookies. I only realized as much once I was halfway down the block and then I was too embarrassed to turn back for them—or maybe I just didn't want to return to the scene where I'd realized the choices I'd made weren't necessarily the ones I should have...

I just needed to walk, to clear my head.

My wandering eventually brought me to a city park that was across from the bus station. Finn's bus still wasn't due to arrive for another hour but I figured I could busy myself by watching children and their parents ice skating in an impromptu ice rink that had been set up over a frozen pond. The space was crowded with families, people drinking hot chocolate while Christmas carols belted out from the tinny speakers.

I settled down on one of the park benches so I could watch the people skating by. The wood was cold underneath me, and I kept my hands tucked into my pockets to keep them warm. It was adorable to watch all the little kids skating in their brightly colored snowsuits. The littlest ones looked like starfish, their puffy jackets holding their arms and legs out to the side. Some teens streaked by, kicking up a wave of frost in their wake, while an older couple, their gray heads bent together, glided by serenely.

My eyes caught on a couple with a small boy, his blond curls just barely peeking out from below his wool hat. They each held one of his hands as he slowly, determinedly, inched his way around the pond. His little tongue poked out in concentration as he shuffled his feet forward. Of course, the child reminded me of Finn at that age—they both had the same white-blond hair and pink cheeks.

From the wide smiles on their faces, both parents were encouraging him as he picked his way forward. While I watched, they shared a glance over their son's head, and the father leaned forward to steal a quick kiss from his wife.

I turned away, a little pang running through my chest.

How different my life had turned out.

When you're a little girl, you think Prince Charming will come riding up on his white steed to take you away to your own Happily Ever After. But then in adulthood, you come to realize that all of that is just a pipe dream.

Only if you marry the wrong man.

The thought interjected itself into my brain like the blade of a knife and even though the voice was my own, it still felt foreign.

I breathed in deeply and forced myself to pay attention to the scene around me—I just couldn't face my own thoughts at the moment. Across the way, a young woman was sitting on a bench like mine and looked like she was having an even worse day than I was. She was huddled into her coat, obviously miserable, and I was pretty sure the red in her nose and cheeks was from crying, not just the nipping cold.

My mom instincts raised their head as I wondered what in the world could have happened that would have made this young woman so upset. No one should be alone on a park bench crying on Christmas Eve. Was she okay? Did she need help? I was getting ready to stand, to try and come up with some excuse to walk over and check on her, when a young man walked up to her and sat down beside her.

It took a minute for the girl to even notice he was there, and then she seemed a little embarrassed that someone was witnessing her sadness, but the young man just smiled and struck up what looked like a casual conversation with her and pretty soon she was smiling and a second later, a laugh bubbled up and out of her.

I was still debating walking over to make sure everything was okay, but something held me in place on my bench. I couldn't hear what they were talking about since they were too far away, and the sounds of the people skating were too loud. But as I watched, some life crept back into the girl's face. After a few minutes, the young man actually had her laughing out loud.

She'd just looked so unhappy, huddled there in her misery, that the quick turnaround caused my eyes to narrow in suspicion. Especially since it had felt a lot like the two of them were strangers when the young man had first sat down. Watching them now, I started paying closer attention, and as I focused on the pair, I could actually see what was happening.

There were little glimmers of magic working around the young man as he spoke to the girl, unpicking the shadows that hung over her like a shroud. With every word he spoke, she looked a little lighter, a little brighter, less dragged down by whatever was bothering her.

The magic wasn't a type I was familiar with, but just watching the young man work brought a smile to my face. What kind of supernatural was he, to stop and help a stranger feel better on Christmas Eve?

It wasn't that supernatural folk were bad people who wouldn't do a thing like this, but they tended to be pretty insular. They stuck to their own groups, or to the Hollows, and tended to mind their own business so as not to draw too much attention to themselves, and here was this young man who was weaving his magic right out in the open, though to be fair, no mundanes would be able to spot it. I was fairly sure I was the only one who really knew what was going on.

The magic was clearer to me when I

didn't look directly at it, so I took darting glances out of the corner of my eye, trying to place where I might have seen it before. The young man wasn't a warlock, that kind of magic was pretty darn familiar to me after joining Wanda's coven.

He wasn't Fae, either. I'd had far too much exposure to faerie magic in recent months to not be able to identify it. So what was he? It was a mystery.

Whatever he was though, the young man's power was strong. He had a light touch, but I could feel the effervescence of his abilities against my senses, like some of my fizzier potions.

After another minute or so, he said his goodbyes to the young woman on the bench and stood. With his chin tucked down into the collar of his coat, he picked his way through the park, heading in my direction. His head down and his hands in his pockets, I couldn't see much of him other than the blond hair tossed around his face by the wind.

It wasn't until he drew closer and lifted his head to smile at me that I recognized him. And then I sucked in a sharp breath, tears pressing against the corners of my eyes as my heart kicked into overdrive, so full I felt like it might actually burst.

He smiled at me, wide, beloved, and so, so familiar.

Finn.

My son, all grown up and fully come into his power. The magic of a full-blown Magician hung over him like a cloak, brightening the day around him, just as he'd brightened that young woman's day.

"Hi, Mom, I ended up getting an earlier bus—I hope you weren't waiting long," he said, in a voice deeper than I'd ever heard before. "I texted you but never heard back... anyway... Merry Christmas!" Then he threw his arms around me and it was all I could do to keep my tears in check.

***

I spent the car ride back trying to play it cool, which wasn't my strong suit. Fortunately, Finn was used to how I was, so even if he didn't know about the whole 'five years into the future' deal going on, he wasn't put off by the million and one questions I threw at him.

It was so strange, to see my son all grown up. He seemed so mature, such an adult, even at eighteen which was still barely more than a kid. Finn radiated a kind of calm happiness, yet I could still see little flashes of the boy I knew so well. I could still see the boy in the way he smiled, the way he laughed, how he turned to watch things out the window, all of it made my heart ache, but there was a sweetness to it, too—a sweetness to knowing just how wonderful Finn would turn out.

It was nice, having Finn all to myself, even if it was just for the car ride. I got to hear about his school, what classes he was taking, how he was enjoying it, and what he'd been up to. It had been eye-opening to see him in action with the young woman at the park, too. Not only was it clear that my son was still the kind-hearted, compassionate person he'd always been, but it was also a relief to see him so comfortable with his own power and abilities.

Part of the reason I'd dug my heels in so hard regarding Finn learning magic, was because every time he helped someone, he seemed to lose a piece of himself in the process. It was almost like the magic ended up draining him. Magic could be dangerous. I knew that better than most.

Ever since we'd moved to the Hollow, I'd been chased, attacked, and even landed in the hospital a couple of times. Finn himself had been haunted, abducted, and terrified by a mad vampire. I was happy to teach him magic as a way to defend himself, but I was afraid at the same time.

But there was no sign of any weakness or exhaustion in him now as he sat there beside me, chatting and laughing. He sat easily in his seat, just happy to be home for the holidays.

We were about halfway to Haven Hollow when, from the backseat, Finn's bag wriggled. I jumped and fought not to jerk the wheel. "What in the world?"

"Oh, sorry." Finn twisted in his seat, reaching back to undo the zipper on his bag. "I told Ouire he could come out once we were in the car and on the way."

Ouire then wriggled free and squirmed into the front seat with Finn. I had to laugh. The way the book placed the corners of his leather cover on the door, the red ribbon bookmark wagging furiously behind him, Ouire looked like a dog ready to stick his head out the car window.

The book looked well cared for, the gilded edges of his pages gleaming in the sunlight. The leather of his cover looked like Finn might have actually oiled it.

Finn stroked a hand down the book's spine. "Sorry, buddy. I didn't mean to leave you in there so long."

Ouire didn't seem offended, just excited to peek out the widows and sit on Finn's lap. I hoped no one we drove past glanced over to look into the Jeep, because there was no way to explain the book. But I wasn't concerned enough to order the poor book back into Finn's duffel. Truth be told, I was glad Ouire was still a part of Finn's life.

And, of course, seeing Ouire made me think back to my meeting with Andre. My heart gave a painful twinge, but I pushed the feeling away. I couldn't think about that meeting now. I wasn't sure how much more time I had in this scenario (and hoped upon hope I wasn't stuck here indefinitely, but I had a feeling I wouldn't be—that this little trip into the future was the exact gift Noelle said it would be—a gift to allow me to make a decision in my own time that would affect the rest of my life).

And that was something I could think about later. For now, Finn was growing up before my eyes, present or future, and any time I got to spend with him was precious. I didn't want to waste any of it worrying about other things.

Because the truth was that none of it mattered. All that did matter was right here and right now. The rest... well, the rest I could figure out later.

Chapter Seven

Somehow, I remembered to pick up eggs once we reached Haven Hollow, and Finn, who at six-foot-three now towered over me, carried the grocery bag inside for me.

He whistled for Ouire, who was bounding around in the snow as Finn shouldered the door open. "Hey, come on, buddy. Don't get your pages wet."

I had to laugh, watching the book shake itself and race into the house like an excited puppy.

I closed the door behind us and started peeling off my winter layers as Finn set his duffle bag down.

Marty came out of the kitchen then, wiping his hands on a dish towel. His face split into a wide grin, eyes crinkling up as soon as he saw Finn. Then the two were crossing the distance that separated them and hugging one another.

"Finn!" Marty all but sang. "I can't wait to hear all your college stories! You got a girlfriend yet?"

"Not yet," Finn managed with a shy smile as Marty thunked him on the back and then directed him to the kitchen.

"It's just a matter of time with a mug like that! Hey, you're just in time for my world-famous eggnog!"

"I thought that's why I was picking up eggs?" I called out as Finn gave me a look that said he disliked Marty's 'world-famous eggnog' as much as I did.

"Nah, I just used the ones you had in the fridge so it's a good thing you got more!"

In spite of everything, all my doubts and worries, seeing Marty with his arm slung around Finn's shoulder as they headed into the kitchen, brought a warmth to my chest like summer sunlight.

Even so, I still couldn't help but feel like

something was missing.

***

It was a wonderful night, with far too much food and movies and cuddling under the blankets. We watched all our holiday favorites, and Marty and Finn ganged up on me until I finally relented and we watched Die Hard.

All the while, I pushed away my doubts, but they kept creeping back in—seemingly whenever my mind wasn't focused on something else. It was like the shadows in the corners of your bedroom as a kid—just waiting to make themselves known when you're not paying attention.

Even though I loved watching Finn with Marty and witnessing the incredible man my son had become, there was still a strange hollowness to my joy, aching and empty like a missing tooth I just couldn't stop prodding with my tongue.

Eventually we all turned in, Finn to his old room and Marty and me to ours. Marty fell asleep almost instantly, the bed trembling with the sound of his snores. It was only then that I realized I still wasn't wearing my rings—they were out in the center consul of the Jeep.

I lay awake for a long time, staring at the familiar ceiling of my room. I just couldn't get my mind to quiet, my thoughts racing around inside my head like a dog chasing its own tail. Something close to dread built inside my chest, weighing down my lungs and making it hard to breathe.

Lying there in the dark, watching the red numbers on my alarm clock ticking over was almost unbearable. It wasn't until they flipped to midnight, Christmas Day, that my eyelids finally slid closed and I fell into a fitful sleep.

When I opened my eyes again, it was morning.

The first faint traces of dawn outside were sneaking through my curtains and painting the ceiling with soft gray light. Everything was still, and quiet. It was the kind of hush that only winter mornings have, when the snow outside muffles the whole world.

The quiet tipped me off, but I craned my neck to the side just to check. Sure enough, the other side of my bed was empty, with no sign of Marty anywhere. The sheets on that side were cool to the touch, and I sagged back against the bed with something that was a little too close to relief.

"What a dream," I said to myself even as I shook my head and wondered if it really was a dream. It just... well, if it was just a dream then it was the most realistic dream I'd ever had.

When I shifted my head, something crinkled in my hair, and I sat up in surprise. Whatever it was had slipped between the pillows, and it took me a minute to fish it back out again in the pre-dawn light.

But once I did fish it out, I had to smile. It was a candy cane, one of those from Sweeter Haunts, all wrapped up with a red satin ribbon tied into a perfect bow. A little gift card hung off the ribbon, and when I twisted it around and squinted at it, I could make out the words *'To Poppy, Merry Christmas'* written on it in beautiful calligraphy.

Even though there was no mention of the gift giver, I knew.

Noelle.

I fell back onto my pillows, the candy cane clutched to my chest.

Then, thinking better of it, I bolted upright and ran over to the mirror hanging on the wall. And what I saw there made me smile—no extra wrinkles or extra grays in sight. I sagged against the wall, my forehead pressed against the cool glass.

Glancing down at the candy cane in my hand, I could only laugh as I pieced together the puzzle—that had been no dream. I'd been visited by the Spirit of Christmas and granted a vision into a possible future. I was fairly sure that's exactly what had happened and I couldn't say I was *that* surprised. This was Haven Hollow, after all—a place where the extraordinary was commonplace.

So now the question was: was the life I'd just witnessed—the future that lay before me if I chose to stay with Marty—was it the life I wanted? It was a good life, comfortable and affectionate even, but I hadn't grown to love Marty passionately and truthfully, I couldn't say that he seemed all that passionately in love with me, either. Instead, it had appeared like we'd just sort of plateaued.

So I had to wonder: how much did passion mean to me? How important was it to be *in love* with someone versus just loving them? And what about passion fading?

No.

The word just sort of shotgunned through my head.

No.

No. No. No.

NO!

I couldn't marry Marty.

The truth just sort of beat me over the head as I stood standing there in front of my bedroom mirror, candy cane clutched to my chest.

Whether I'd had a Christmas wish granted or not, the answer was obvious.

It didn't matter if it faded; it didn't matter if it wasn't the safe choice: I wanted passion.

I wanted sparks, and romance and butterflies every time I thought of the man I loved.

And that wasn't going to happen if I continued down the road I was currently on. More than that—this indecision and reluctance and fear—none of it was fair to Marty.

He deserved more. He deserved someone who was crazy about him, who was eager and excited by the idea of marrying him.

And I just couldn't give him that.

I had to break it off. It was as simple as that.

And the sooner the better.

Of course, I didn't like to think about it because breaking it off meant breaking Marty's heart and he was the last person I would ever want to hurt. But I also didn't want to lead him on and make him think I loved him the way he wanted me to. That was worse.

No, the Band-Aid needed to be yanked off so the healing could start.

And with some luck, and maybe a Christmas miracle or two, we'd be able to get back to where we were before all the other stuff started happening. Hopefully someday we could be friends again, just the way we had been when I'd first moved to Haven Hollow.

It might have been selfish of me, but I didn't want to lose one of my best friends.

Feeling both guilty, and strangely light, I made my way quietly down the stairs to put on a pot of coffee and to start pulling Christmas breakfast together.

I'd just finished mixing up the pancake

batter, when there was the sound of feet on the stairs, and Finn burst into the kitchen, grinning widely.

"Merry Christmas, Mom!" He hurried across the kitchen and flung his arms around me.

A little startled, I shoved the bowl back onto the counter before I dropped it, and then happily returned the hug.

I smoothed Finn's hair off his forehead, and pulled him away as I beamed up at him. Looking into his big, blue eyes, I saw a glimpse of the man he'd become even if the soft, rounded lines of his face seemed to be-lie that truth. Even as I fought against them, tears burned at the corners of my eyes, and I had to blink a few times to push them back.

Time was passing.

Finn was growing up, getting older with each and every day.

But for now, for this moment, I had my son in my arms, and that was the best sort of present.

I planted a kiss on his forehead, and he didn't even grumble.

"Merry Christmas, Finn."

***

After all the madness of Christmas morning, once presents were opened, breakfast was eaten, and things were at least partially cleaned up, Finn offhandedly mentioned that some of his friends from school were planning on doing some tobogganing at one of the bigger hills in town. I could tell by the overly casual way he brought the topic up that he was gauging how I felt about it before outright asking. I had to press my lips together to keep from smiling.

"Do you want to go with them?"

"Is that okay?"

"Sure… as long as you're back before dinner."

Finn's head shot up, his eyes shining. "Really?"

I did smile then. 'Really', he was asking me. As though he hadn't been a walking lie detector since he was just out of diapers. My son might have been growing into being a Magician, but he was born of Scottish Traveller blood, and that magic had come to him first.

"Of course," I said, flattening one last

box. "Have fun, and be careful. Just be home before dark. Don't forget, your uncles are coming for dinner."

"Yes! Thanks, Mom, you're the best." Finn gave me another hug before hurrying to put his coat on.

Normally, we spent the whole of Christmas day together. But holding Finn back wouldn't help anything—especially when he obviously wanted to play in the snow with his friends. Part of me wanted to make him stay home though, like I could hoard the time I still had while he was young.

But truthfully, letting Finn go out with his friends was a teeny bit selfish. Because I just needed a little space to clear my mind. It had been really stressful, spending the morning with Marty while coming to terms with what I knew I had to do. Lucky for me, Finn was distracted by everything holiday related and wasn't paying close attention to Marty and me. That would have been a horrible time for his lie detecting ability to kick in, before I'd had a chance to even speak with Marty. Or with Finn. I didn't want to hurt anyone, but whether it was Christmas magic, or my own subconscious, I knew a future with Marty wouldn't make me happy.

So once Finn was out the door, calling out one last promise not to be late, and after I had the turkey in the oven, I decided to go for a walk to clear my head.

Chapter Eight

It was the perfect Christmas day, with a gentle snow falling from fluffy silver clouds in the pale sky. Everything was quiet and still, almost serene. I walked aimlessly, just breathing deeply of the chilly air, and letting my thoughts wander along with my feet.

Haven Hollow was a small town, so I wasn't worried about getting lost. And, eventually, I'd have to go back to the house to baste the turkey, but for right now, I really needed the chance to think.

I knew ending things with Marty was the right thing to do. Not just for me, but for him. I wanted both of us to be happy, not just content. That didn't make the decision one bit easier, though. I really hated hurting people's feelings and especially the people who were closest to me.

Eventually, I wandered down the street that Fifi lived on. Just as I was rounding the corner, Fifi's front door opened and she and Roy stepped out.

Then Fifi caught sight of me. "Merry Christmas, Poppy!"

I waved back, grinning. "Merry Christmas to you both!"

Roy slung a casual arm around Fifi's waist and I remembered the visual of both of them standing outside the Half-Moon, happy as can be, with their new baby. The memory or the thought or whatever it was, made me smile.

Fifi tensed at Roy's arm snaking around her waist, like she thought I'd be mad at Roy for showing her affection in front of me. I'd gotten the impression that she'd been worried about dating Roy for a while after he and I broke up, thinking that in doing so, she'd hurt me. Fifi really was too sweet to be a demon. Yes, the breakup had stung for a bit, even if I knew it was the right thing to do, but I was glad to see them both so happy.

"Do you want to stop in for coffee?" Roy asked.

I kept my smile in place and my voice light, trying to show her that their PDA didn't bother me at all. The truth was—it didn't. "Thank you, but I should be heading home. I've got a turkey that needs tending. I just wanted to take a quick walk."

"All right, then," Roy said with an easy smile. "Don't be a stranger."

I waved to them and they disappeared back inside the house.

Strangely, seeing Roy made me feel a little bit better about things. He hadn't been happy about our breakup, either, but really, even if I hadn't been given a heads up about Fifi being his soulmate, I was pretty sure we wouldn't have worked out long term. For one thing, at eighty, Roy was young for a Sasquatch. I was over forty, and aging like any other human. By the time I was old and gray, Roy would look like he was my grandson. Plus, Sasquatch tended to have big families, and I knew Roy wanted kids, but Finn was plenty for me.

Roy and I—we just hadn't been meant to be. And the situation between us hadn't been great right after the breakup, but Roy and I had managed to get our friendship back pretty quickly, and Roy had moved on to find the love of his life. And that fact gave me hope that Marty would do the same. That not only would he and I be okay, in the end, but that in freeing him, he'd be able to find the woman he was truly supposed to be with.

And yes, seeing Roy and Fifi together maybe made me a tiny bit jealous. Just a little. Not that I was jealous about Fifi being with Roy, but I was a little envious over what they had together. Their relationship, and how well they meshed as a couple. That was what I wanted, and I could now admit it to myself.

The future wasn't set in stone, wasn't that what Noelle had told me? That our choices could change things. Nothing was pre-determined and we could change the shape of our paths. So, did that mean that visual of Fifi and Roy with their baby was something that might not happen? I figured it did.

Roy and Fifi's future was up to them to decide—just as mine was up to me. And for some reason, that thought brought a skip to my stride.

My feet brought me to Main Street, and I figured I'd take a walk past my shop before heading home to finish dinner preparations. Maybe it was cheating, but in my mind, I was already playing around with some of the new additions I'd seen in my shop in the dreamscape.

A gust of chilly wind and snow tickled the back of my neck, and I shivered as I stuffed my hands further down into my coat pockets. Under my fingers, something crinkled, and I frowned until I pulled out the candy cane that had been sitting on my pillow this morning.

I had to laugh a little. As far as Christmas wishes went, this was kind of a tough one. Even so, I felt at peace with my decision, come what may. I knew I'd be saving both me and Marty a lot of heartache down the road, and I'd just have to take the consequences as they came.

I stood on the sidewalk outside of Poppy's Potions, under the twinkling Christmas lights, and tilted my head back to let the gentle snowflakes land on my cheeks.

"Thank you, Noelle," I murmured to the wind, and I wasn't just referencing the candy cane in my hand.

I'd never had anything from Sweeter Haunts that was less than delectable, and I figured I could use a bit of a treat, it was Christmas, after all, so I tugged the silky red ribbon free from the candy cane and started unwrapping it.

With my head down, and my attention occupied, I didn't realize there was anyone else on the sidewalk until I plowed head first into them.

"Oh my gosh, I'm so sorry! I wasn't looking where I was going." The words came tumbling out on automatic as I tried to jerk back. Somehow, the ribbon from the candy cane had gotten tangled around the other person's hand, and I had to fight the urge not to yank it back in mortification. "Sorry!"

"Poppy?"

I jerked my chin up to stare into Andre's surprised face. Heat flooded my cheeks as a blush climbed up from my neck. Of course, I couldn't have crashed into just anyone, it had to be Alixandre Osmont, the focus of all my most confused and embarrassing thoughts.

"H-h-hi," I managed, sounding out of breath and flustered.

He glanced down at his hand and mine and the red ribbon that was now decidedly wrapped around both of them. I frowned as I tried to understand how that was possible—how had the ribbon leapt from my candy cane and wrapped itself around Andre's hand? Andre didn't seem to be concerned with it though and, instead, rubbed his fingers over my left finger, where Marty's engagement ring was decidedly missing. I'd taken it off as soon as I'd reached my decision and put it in the top drawer of my nightstand.

"Will you look at that?" Andre asked as a little smirk caught his mouth—I wasn't sure if he was referring to my missing engagement ring or the red ribbon that had wound itself around both of our hands.

I didn't know what to say. I didn't know how to act. All I could see was the slightly older version of him saying how much he regretted never speaking up, never telling me how he felt about me and more importantly, that he felt for me the same way I did for him. Doubt then rang through me as I wondered whether the vision was a true picture of the future, or just the wishful thinking of my subconscious?

It was real, I told myself. *You know it was real.*

One thing that was for sure—the attraction I felt for Andre was still firmly in place. The sense of rightness, of familiarity, as if some part of me had breathed out in relief to have our hands touching. It was a little embarrassing, really.

And that darn ribbon still wouldn't come untangled.

Andre's fingers tightened on mine, and he calmly unwound the red ribbon from our fingers before offering it to me with a smile. "Are you alright?"

"I'm fine." I took the ribbon with a shaky laugh and stuffed it back into my pocket, along with the candy cane. "Are you alright? I walked right into you kind of hard."

He smiled, looking so smart and dapper in his charcoal wool coat, his scarf folded around his neck. "I'm okay, thank you," he said and his voice was a little sad. "Happy Christmas, by the way."

Something relaxed inside me at the sight of that smile, going warm and soft. "Merry Christmas, Andre. What brings you to Haven Hollow?"

We hadn't spoken after Thanksgiving night, after Marty had asked me to marry him and I'd said yes. I'd just assumed Andre had returned to Portland to tend to whatever business he had there and that he'd remained. Seeing him here now? Well, it was surprising to say the least.

His shoulders rose and fell in an easy shrug. "I was feeling restless, and needed to clear my head."

"Me too," I laughed. "But I meant—what are you doing in Haven Hollow? I haven't spoken to you since—" I couldn't even bring myself to complete the sentence.

"Since you got engaged?" he asked with a strange smile.

"Right."

Then he seemed to pause for a moment or so. "Are you... still engaged?" He glanced down at the missing ring from my finger.

"That's a complicated topic that I'd, um, rather not get into at the moment," I admitted. I wanted to discuss this whole situation with Marty before I discussed it with anyone else.

Andre nodded as if he understood and didn't press the topic, which I appreciated. "As to why I'm in Haven Hollow," he started and then cocked his head to the side as a light snow started to dust the two of us in gentle flakes. "I live here."

I couldn't help my surprise at that. "You... you live here?"

He nodded. "I do."

I frowned, not understanding how that was possible. "Then you bought a house?"

"I did," he answered with a quick nod. "Do you recall the one we toured together?"

"The one just up the road?"

He'd been looking into the farmhouse a few doors down from my own, and he'd invited me to go and take a look at it with him. It had been a gorgeous place, quite a bit bigger than my own, and in need of fewer renovations to boot, but I hadn't thought he'd settled on it yet.

Andre nodded, looking pleased. "I'm in the process of moving in."

I couldn't help the sense of warmth that suddenly suffused me. And not only for myself. "Finn's going to be over the moon," I said with a big smile. "You know, he hasn't said anything, but I noticed a new number on his arm the other day."

Finn had latched onto Andre quickly, seeing him as something of a cool, mysterious teacher, I suspected. It was going to be wonderful having Andre around to help keep Finn from burning himself out as he learned to be a Magician. Maybe between the two of us, we'd be able to protect Finn from himself long enough for him to grow into the thoughtful, kind-hearted, powerful young man I'd seen in my vision.

And, if there were other reasons it might be nice to have Andre so close, living in the Hollow, then that was something I could think about later. A lot later.

"He's mastered another trick already?" Andre gave a low whistle. "The boy's a prodigy. It's not surprising, considering who his mother is."

The flush that had been finally dying

down flared back to life, and I had to force myself not to duck my head like a school girl. "You give me too much credit."

One dark brow arched, but Andre's smile never faltered. "I think you give yourself too little, but I'll agree to disagree."

I wanted to ask him a thousand questions. They were burning at the back of my tongue; I didn't even know where to start. Did he know anyone else in town? Did he have anywhere to go for Christmas? I couldn't bear the thought of him alone, but it would look a little odd if I invited him to our house, especially given the state of my relationship with Marty.

Before I could sort through the tangle of thoughts snared in my head, a particularly bitter gust of wind came tearing down the street and actually made me stagger forward a step to keep my balance.

Wide eyed, Andre caught me before I went any further, and the press of his gloved hands on my arm was somehow warm, even through my coat.

"This might not be the place to have a chat," he said, a little ruefully. "I don't suppose you have time to get a Christmas coffee and catch up a little?"

I couldn't help but recall that in the Christmas vision courtesy of Noelle, he'd asked something similar—asking to catch up after five years. Taking a deep breath, I pulled my phone out of my pocket and noted it was earlier than I'd thought it was. I had a bit of time before I needed to baste the bird, so I nodded, feeling pleased. "Sure, that sounds good."

We fell in step with each other, shoulders brushing as we walked. It felt good. It felt right. Like I'd been hobbling around, but suddenly I could take a proper step again.

The strange sense of familiarity didn't feel so worrisome, now that I knew there was a chance that Andre felt it too—well, from what he'd admitted to me in my vision, anyway. That deep sense of déjà vu had frightened me a little, when we'd first met. I hadn't understood where it was coming from. I still didn't, but it was one of those things that just felt less scary when it was shared.

I tilted my head back to the sky, as the snow fell gently around us, flakes landing on my skin like little icy kisses. The whole day had been so perfect so far, that it felt a bit like I'd been given a gift.

The wrapper in my pocket crinkled slightly.

"Actually, I don't think I'll get a coffee," I started, after we'd walked a few steps.

"No?"

I shook my head and smiled up at him. "I think today calls for a candy cane hot chocolate."

I laughed, the fog of my breath pluming on the air. "I'm in the mood for something festive."

The End

~~~~~~

Return to Haven Hollow in:
Georgian Ghouls
Haven Hollow #26
(Hallowed Homes)
by J.R. Rain and H.P. Mallory

If you enjoyed *The Christmas Spirit,* please

help spread the word by leaving a review!
Thank you!

Also available:
Don't miss the release of the first book in a
brand new paranormal women's fiction series!
Shotguns and Shifters
Trailer Park Vampire #1
by J.R. Rain and H.P. Mallory

(read on for a sample)

Chapter One

Waitressing had been hard enough *before*
the fog rolled in.

The Damnation Diner was the only de-
cent restaurant this side of the Ozarks, and
now, instead of Budweiser, we served blood.
And blood didn't keep *nearly* as well as
booze.

I walked along the sterile aisles, shuffling
in my worn, leather heels from table to table.
Gathering up some orders, I chatted with the
locals about the specials, all the things a normal waitress does. The only difference was
that breakfast in the Damnation Diner was
usually served right about midnight and the

people I was serving, to put it bluntly, weren't people at all.

'The Fog', as we came to call it, was a deep red mist that had settled over our little town of Windy Ridge. It had spread everywhere within a hundred-mile radius, and when it came, none of us knew what to make of it, much less what to do about it.

Some folk thought the Rapture was upon us—the two churches on either side of town were full to the brim. But when the first people began to change, those thoughts got stamped out right quick.

The changes started slow, with neighbors screaming in their homes, apparently losing their dang minds, then running out into the woods, never to be seen again. Those that *were* seen again didn't fare much better— some of them started sprouting horns, others tails, some now had claws, and others, fur. We even found some with gills but, unfortunately, we couldn't get them to water in time.

I still have nightmares about that.

Overall, there was sheer and utter panic, people yelling and praying as they slowly began to shift into unthinkable things, but no one knew what was happening. The only thing we did know, the only thing we could attribute the horror to, was the burnt, blood-colored clouds that had floated into our town and then floated right back on out again. That danged fog had changed everyone and everything in Windy Ridge. And it had only taken a week to do it.

It's hard to believe that those fairy tale monsters you hear about as kids are actually real—well, that is until you wake up and see dryads frolicking through the trailers and swamp creatures soaking in kiddie pools as they wave to you with newly webbed hands.

Yep, that red fog had affected every one of us, but not in the same way. The only person in town that hadn't changed into a full-bodied creature was Boone, and that was only 'cause the fog had cured the lung cancer that was slowly and mercilessly killing him. Not only that, but the fog also left him with a keen invulnerability to any kind of harm.

Like I said, *everyone* had changed, and I wasn't immune. One day I woke up to a ray of sunshine peeking on through my trailer window and let me tell you, that ray of light felt like the devil's own poison once it hit my skin. Next thing I knew? My mouth was full of blood.

Naturally, I panicked and rushed to the restroom, only to find I'd grown fangs which had gone and left two holes in my bottom lip. Only once I caught my breath and forcibly told myself to calm down did I realize my blood tasted like the gods' very own nectar. Thankfully, everything else about my appearance stayed pretty much the same, except for the fact that the years stopped hitting me and I had two pinprick scars underneath my lower lip. When normies came around (which wasn't often), I said the scars were from old piercings.

Technically, I wasn't fibbing.

I was never one for old folks' tales, but that didn't mean I couldn't guess what I'd turned into. I could run like hell and any injury I had was healed within a minute. I had superhuman strength, couldn't stand the sun, and I'd stopped aging. And I had a hankering for blood that was one hundred times as strong as the worst craving you ever had during shark week.

Yep, I'd gone vampy.

And that was when I realized that everything I thought I knew about bloodsuckers was wrong. Well, *almost* everything. For one thing—that whole bit about vampires fearing crosses? A bucket of horse manure. I can still pop by the local Baptist church and not even flinch. My reflection still looks back at me in the mirror whenever I'm in a visiting sort of mood and I have to admit, I look better than I have in years. My hair's as red as it was when I was a girl, and those heavy baby diapers that used to hang under my eyes? Now a thing of the past. In fact, all my age lines disappeared the day I grew fangs and the chicken pox scars Ma (rest her soul) described as giving me 'character' now are nowhere to be found.

I could still handle garlic, both in salt and bulb form, and, thank *God,* there was no fear of running water that kept me from showering. The oddest thing, though, was that I wasn't actually *dead.* My heart still beat, chugging on like a determined engine in a worn-out, old Ford. And I definitely hadn't passed away to awaken as a walking corpse Nosferatu style with an oversized head, ridiculously long fingernails and bucked-teeth fangs. In fact, near as I could tell, I never actually died.

My daughter, Sicily (the smartest of us), believes there's some kind of scientific explanation for everything that happened. She chalked up my blood hunger to a severe vitamin deficiency and who knows? Maybe that's it. That girl is smarter than I could ever be, so I usually leave the theories to her. I don't know if we'll ever find out exactly what happened the day that fog rolled in, but the good thing about Windy Ridge is that its people are resilient. We adapted, and now, life almost feels like normal again.

I grabbed a fresh batch of chicken tenders (uncooked and minus the breading) from the kitchen and shouldered my way out through the double doors, striding over to a table that usually fit four but was now encompassed entirely by one man. I'm comfortable saying 'man' because he did still have *some* human features, like the large feet that spread out beneath the table (even if they were covered in course, brown hair) and the nose that sniffed the food as I put it down. But that nose wasn't quite human, elongated as it was.

Bud reminded me of Barf, John Candy's dog character from Space Balls. He had that sorta look and was overlarge, probably the largest creature in town (I'd guess him to be over six-foot-five), with long, shaggy brown hair, and eyes that betrayed his kindness. His arms matched the color of his hair and were patched with the same fur that covered the rest of him. When he grinned at me, he revealed a set of powerful canine teeth. Reaching for the chicken with his paws, he curled his claws around one of them and gave me a great big grin.

"Summa bitch, Twila, I'm gonna need me three more orders!" he said as he glanced down at the chicken tenders which were piled high on the plate in front of him.

"I'm gonna have to charge you for more, Bud," I informed him.

He nodded, before looking up at me. "What aboutta trade?"

I cocked my head to the side. "Whattdya got for me?"

"I caught me something that used to be a deer out in my traps early this morning."

I nodded. We were getting low on meat. "Sure—that should do." Then I tapped him on his big, furry shoulder. "You enjoy your breakfast now, Bud."

"Thank you, Twila, m'dear."

I smiled, watching him tear into the chicken with gusto. He snorted, wiping food out from his beard (and a wolf with a beard is a definite site to see) and rested his elbows on the table, just like he had before he'd turned into a wolfman.

"You gonna show up to the meetin' today?" Bud called out to me when I was about to walk away. "Ol' Ned's been workin' on his trap sketches. You oughta see what he's gotten up to."

I pursed my lips and sighed—the 'meeting' Bud was talking about was a get-together of the local monster hunters in town, and I wasn't excited to be included among them. "I guess."

Bud looked up at me. "It's right important you show up, Twila. You're a valuable member o' our team, you are."

I nodded, because I'd missed their last three meetings and I did feel a certain level of guilt. "After I make sure Sicily's settled."

"Feel free to bring 'er," Bud said, and I caught the excited glint in his eye before he could hide it. "Maybe she'll find somethin' interestin'."

"Quit tryin' to squeeze the smart outta my daughter." I grinned, shaking my head as I patted him on the shoulder again. I'd known Bud all my life, which wasn't that unusual since I'd been born in Windy Ridge, but he was still like an older brother to me. "I'll let you know after my shift. Promise."

Bud nodded, mouth full of poultry, and I continued on to the rest of my patrons. I passed by a stony-looking man who was sitting in a booth three down from Bud and slid him his coffee. 'Stony' was a good description, seeing as how his skin was fine granite and gray wings sprouted from his back (he kept them folded while inside the diner). Stony didn't sip the coffee, instead, he brought it to his nose for a long sniff. Probably still aching for the caffeine even if his intestines were now made out of rock.

The plate I was holding—one full of dirt, leaves, and twigs—I handed to a pretty faun woman who was sitting beside the potted plants at the back of the joint. She gave me a relieved smile as she took it, eyeing the large fronds of the fern with definite hunger.

Something wet dropped on my shoulder, and I looked up to see the man-bat hanging from one of the diner's fluorescent lights. He flashed me an apologetic smile as he licked the juice which was still falling from his lips.

"You gotta get you some real OJ, Twila," he said as he looked at me and shook his head.

"It ain't the season for oranges, Cletus," I answered. "You know that."

"This Sunny D shit's gonna 'cause the death of me."

"It's the closest thing to orange juice we got."

I walked on by as my attention caught on the figure hunched in the corner booth, her head hidden by a mountain of thick text-books. Now she was probably the most un-conventional creature in Windy Ridge.

A brown-haired human I knew as my daughter.

I grinned at Sicily and finished up the rest of my orders before sliding into the booth opposite her with a plate of food. She didn't look up, and that special frown of hers was fully in place—one that only appeared when she was deeply entrenched in a new book. The girl read more than everyone in Windy Ridge combined—which might have not been saying much 'cause I was fairly sure a good portion of the population couldn't read at all.

She jumped when I shoved the toasted ravioli under her nose, followed swiftly by a large glass of water. "Y'know you still have to eat, right?" I asked in my best Ma tone. "If you don't keep your strength up, something else is gonna end up eatin' *you.*"

Sicily laughed and made a face at me in reply. "Nah. I can just call for you and you'll take care of them before they get to me."

"I'm not able to pop outta thin air, Sicily," I said, tapping the plate with my finger. "Eat."

She rolled her eyes, but then did as I'd ordered. I, meanwhile, took a glance at the cover of her book, frowning at the title: *Real Accounts of Fake Monsters.* "I thought we agreed to save the research until *after* your homework was done."

"Homework *is* done," Sicily said with a mouthful of *I'm not telling the truth.* I raised my eyebrow.

"Sicily."

"Okay, okay, I didn't do it yet." She folded her arms, gesturing to the book. "But c'mon, Mama, this is *way* more important than calculus. What we're dealing with could change evolution as we know it."

"Yeah, well, I'll be sure to tell that to Darwin next time he's in town."

"I'm serious, Mama. What if that fog comes back?"

It was the question everyone in town had been asking since the fog came and went. Since it had been over a year, I didn't think it was a worry we needed to have any longer. "You know as well as I do that that darned fog isn't coming back."

It was almost funny that the only human left in this town was more interested in the fog's origins than anyone else. Sicily had been at her father's when the fog rolled into town (and then rolled back out just as fast), so she wasn't affected. I've still never been more thankful for anything in my life.

"We don't know for sure," she argued.

"While that might be true," I began, taking a math textbook from the pile and plopping it beside her plate. "My hand is gonna have a lot more impact on your backside if you don't hop to it."

That got her to smile again (mostly because I'd never laid a hand on her and never would), and she nodded sarcastically, scooping up more ravioli and prying the book's pages open. I sat back, watching her reluctantly glance at her math homework, and somewhere in my chest, I felt my heart ache just a bit.

Sicily took after her father, with his brown hair and eyes instead of the messy red nest that sat atop my head, and for good and for bad, she reminded me of him whenever I really got a good look at her.

Her father was someone I'd met in Branson, the largest city from Windy Ridge and over two hundred miles away. His name was Alton Reid, a man who'd come from old money but acted as kind as the poorest of us. But that was then and this was now and as my mama used to say—*there weren't no point in dwelling on the past.*

I heard someone calling my name from another table and so I stood up, kissing Sicily on the head before rushing back onto the floor.

When Sicily was born, I'd made a promise to myself to make sure she could leave this place. She could leave and never come back to Windy Ridge if she wanted to—she could make a name and a life for herself somewhere in the big world, maybe Branson or maybe somewhere even bigger. And I would do my damnedest to give her every possibility of freedom and release from this tiny, backwoods town the two of us had grown up in.

But God must have a bad sense of humor, because all Sicily wanted to do was stay. Stay and find out what in tarnation was going on in Windy Ridge. She wanted to find out why everyone had changed when the fog rolled in, why *I'd* changed.

But the last thing I wanted was for her to stay here, trapped in this town because of me.

Shotguns and Shifters
now available at Amazon!

About J.R. Rain

J.R. Rain is the international bestselling author of over seventy novels, including his popular Samantha Moon and Jim Knighthorse series. His books are published in five languages in twelve countries, and he has sold more than 3 million copies worldwide.

Please find him at: www.jrrain.com.

About H.P. Mallory

H.P. Mallory is a New York Times and USA Today bestselling author. She has eleven series currently and she writes paranormal fiction, heavy on the romance! H.P. lives in Southern California with her son and a cranky cat.

To learn more about H.P. and to download free books, visit: www.hpmallory.com

Made in the USA
Monee, IL
23 December 2022

23524728R00092